THE CHERRY VALLEY MIDDL

DEAR

A LEVEL PLAYING FIELD

by RACHEL WISE

Simon Spotlight
New York London Toronto Sydney New Delhi

SIMON SPOTLIGHT
An imprint of Simon & Schuster Children's Publishing Division
1230 Avenue of the Americas, New York, New York 10020
Copyright © 2012 by Simon & Schuster, Inc. All rights reserved, including the right of reproduction in whole or in part in any form.
SIMON SPOTLIGHT and colophon are registered trademarks of Simon & Schuster, Inc.
Text by Elizabeth Doyle Carey
Designed by Laura L. DiSiena

For information about special discounts for bulk purchases, please contact Simon & Schuster Special Sales at 1-866-506-1949 or business@simonandschuster.com.
Manufactured in the United States of America 0812 OFF
First Edition 10 9 8 7 6 5 4 3 2 1
ISBN 978-1-4424-5326-5 (pbk)
ISBN 978-1-4424-5384-5 (hc)
ISBN 978-1-4424-5327-2 (eBook)
Library of Congress Control Number 2012943034

Chapter 1

MARTONE AND LAWRENCE: TOGETHER AGAIN!

★ ★ ★

Michael Lawrence is the best-looking boy at Cherry Valley Middle School, and he loves me.

Ha! That got your attention, right? It's what's called a great "lead" in a news article. The first line in any article is the lead, and it's meant to capture the reader's attention right from the start.

I love writing leads almost as much as I love writing headlines. I write headlines in my mind all day, just kind of narrating the action of my life. Headlines are short and snappy and fun to write, but a lead has to really draw you in and make you want to read the entire story.

Unfortunately, this lead is not true. Michael

Lawrence does not love me. Or I don't think he does, anyway. But now that I have your attention, let me flesh out the who, what, when, where, and why of my news story, just as my teachers at journalism camp taught me.

My name is Samantha Martone. I am a student at Cherry Valley Middle School, where I write for our school newspaper, the *Cherry Valley Voice*. I think I'm a pretty normal middle school kid. My best friend since kindergarten is Hailey Jones. My older sister, Allie, goes to high school and is perfect, which is a pain. I live with her and my mom on Buttermilk Lane. I have a really big secret.

The secret is, I am Dear Know-It-All!

Shh! Don't tell anyone!

I guess I should explain who Dear Know-It-All is. Dear Know-It-All writes the advice column in the *Cherry Valley Voice*. Every September, Mr. Trigg, the newspaper's advisor, picks a different person to write the column for the year. And this year he picked me! The only hitch is, you can't tell anyone it's you if you're picked. You have to stay anonymous. Well, actually, there's one other hitch. Writing the column is really hard. Oh, and one *more* major hitch: so is picking which letter you're going to answer in your column each issue.

When things get really hard, I sometimes think of quitting. But honestly, writing the column is kind of interesting, and also, I really, really want to be editor in chief of the *Voice* next year, and quitting Dear Know-It-All would totally take me out of the running.

And most of all, I really like writing a column that everyone in school reads. I mean, it's really the first thing people turn to when the new issue of the *Voice* comes out every other week. And everyone talks about it too.

See, the most gratifying thing for a journalist is to know you're writing interesting stuff that people are reading and talking about. That's why I know in my heart I'll never really quit being Dear Know-It-All.

Oh, I also write regular articles for the paper. I know people read those, too. My best ones are the big investigative pieces I write with my writing partner/lifelong crush, Michael Lawrence.

The good news is that Mr. Trigg thinks we're a great team, so now he assigns us to report together for almost every issue of the paper. The bad news is that Michael is so cute it can be distracting. The other bad news is that he insists on calling me "Pasty," the nickname I got in kindergarten, thanks to a paste-eating incident. (It looked just like vanilla frosting!) And we often disagree on things. He can be annoying sometimes. On the plus side, though, since we work on so many stories together, I get to hang out with Michael Lawrence *a lot*.

Yay!

For example, I'm going to see him in just a few minutes! We're about to have a newspaper staff meeting. Right now I'm in the *Voice* office, saving a seat for Michael. But he'll probably be late (as usual) and five different people will ask if anyone is sitting in the seat I'm saving, and when I say yes, they'll scowl at me and then he'll get here so late that he won't even be able to get from the door to the seat I've saved. I usually try to sit near the door so he can just quietly slink in and sit next to me, but somebody else always seems to get to that seat first. If only Michael could get here on time for once in his life! See what I mean? I'm annoyed at him already and he's not even here yet. But at least I'll get to hang out with him for a little while afterward. I hope he's wearing something blue today. Blue matches his eyes and makes them really sparkle against his dark hair and tan skin. Swoon!

★ ★ ★

At 3:00 on the dot, Mr. Trigg called the meeting to order and began asking for article ideas. Kids were raising their hands and tossing out topics, and the whole group of us made comments. I love being in the newsroom. The energy, the team feeling, the smell of toner . . . it's a happy place.

I had finally given up and released Michael's seat to an eighth grader when he snuck in the door and quietly pulled it shut behind him. He looked over at me and raised his eyebrows in greeting, then looked around the room. It gave me an extra second to check him out, which is my favorite pastime.

Tall, long legs, dark wavy hair, bright blue eyes, a dark BLUE (yes!) short-sleeve T-shirt over a long-sleeve light BLUE (yes!!) shirt, plus tan corduroys all add up to major cuteness! He glanced back at me in his scan of the room, and I looked away, blushing for getting caught staring at him. He crossed his arms and leaned against the door, biting his lower lip in a serious, Brad Pitt kind of way. I could see his arm muscles through his sleeves. Sigh.

Michael is a major jock. He plays varsity football in the fall and varsity basketball in the winter, and he is cocaptain (with an eighth grader!) of the varsity baseball team in the spring. All of this contributes to his hunky bod and graceful coordination. I, on the other hand, am so not a jock. I am a superklutz and not even that big of a sports fan. My best friend Hailey is a jock too. She's cocaptain of the girls' varsity soccer team, and she and Michael have this kind of macho jokey athletic relationship that sometimes makes me feel jealous and left out. Anyway, I'm more of a bookworm. I love reading and writing and quiet activities, and I don't really see why people think it's so fun to run around and get all sweaty. It seems like a lot of pointless effort to me. I'm just saying.

I turned my attention back to Mr. Trigg, who was going through the week's assignments.

"Righty-ho, we have Susannah on the new safety patrol regulations, Tyler is covering this week's performances of the school concert, Amy is doing a piece on the new Learning Center. I need one more meaty article up front. Any ideas?" He looked around the room. I looked with him. Besides the Dear Know-It-All column I'd have to write, I was fresh out of ideas and hadn't heard anything too inspiring from the crowd today either. Some weeks are just slow news weeks. There's nothing you can do about it.

But then there was Michael, raising his hand.

"Mr. Lawrence, yes?" said Mr. Trigg, adjusting his Union Jack tie. The Union Jack is the British flag. Mr. Trigg is British and is obsessed with World War II, Winston Churchill, and British tabloid newspapers, not necessarily in that order.

Michael cleared his throat. "I heard a rumor

that the school district is going to start charging for after-school sports programs."

Mr. Trigg dropped his tie and raised his eyebrows. "*Really?* That could be *quite* interesting. Where did you hear this?"

"The coaches were talking about it yesterday before practice."

Ho hum, I thought. *Who cares?* I'd pay for our school to *not* have after-school sports. Then I could hang out with Hailey or Michael after school anytime instead of waiting for them to finish running around and getting all grimy.

But Mr. Trigg had folded his arms tightly across his chest and was tapping his chin with his index finger, which is what he always does when he's thinking. "Right. Why don't you and your partner in crime start digging on this one, and let's check back on Wednesday morning and see if we've got a story?"

By "partner in crime," I knew he meant me. I didn't want to smile, but it was hard. Trying to look serious, I nodded at Mr. Trigg, then I turned to look at Michael. He nodded at me and Mr. Trigg.

Martone and Lawrence: Together Again!

I was ecstatic! Not only do I love, love, love Michael Lawrence, I love, love, love writing stories with him. Even though he calls me nicknames, and I usually do klutzy stuff in front of him, and I'm always hungry and my stomach makes a lot of noise when it rumbles . . . except for all that, I *love* working with Michael Lawrence.

I imagined another headline: *Martone and Lawrence: A Modern-Day Woodward and Bernstein!*

Woodward and Bernstein were the famous journalists who reported some illegal stuff President Nixon was doing in the 1970s. Nixon ended up resigning because of what they reported. Anyway, Woodward and Bernstein were, like, the best investigative reporters ever, and I want to be just like them.

When the meeting broke up, Michael was waiting for me by the door. "How's it going, Pasty?" he asked.

Ugh. I bet Woodward never called Bernstein "Pasty."

"Good, Mikey," I replied, calling him by the family nickname that I once heard his mom use. Two could play at this game.

"All right, that's enough of that," he said, but he was grinning.

I grinned back.

"So how do we get started?" I said.

"Let's meet at lunch tomorrow to brainstorm. I've gotta run to football right now."

I rolled my eyes. "All play and no work makes Mikey a dull boy," I teased.

He smiled. "I think you've got that backward."

"No, I don't, Mikey. I really don't."

He laughed as he walked away, and I tried not to swoon.

Chapter 2

MARTONE A BORN WALLFLOWER

★ ★ ★

Hailey came over after soccer practice so I could help her with her homework as usual. She is dyslexic and gets some help from a tutor the school district provides, but she prefers to work with me when she can. I don't mind. By the time she gets here after soccer, I've usually finished most of my other homework anyway.

We followed our usual routine: I offered Hailey a snack. She declined. I made myself a snack. Hailey ate it. Then we got down to business. Talking about boys, that is.

"I get to write another article with superhunk!" I cried.

Hailey was munching on a cracker with melted

cheddar cheese. "What else is new?" she said, spraying crumbs all over her plate. "Oops!" She laughed, spraying some more.

I rolled my eyes. "Why 'what else is new'?" I asked.

"You guys are totally a team at this point. It's like . . . a given that you write everything together. You're like . . . peanut butter and jelly. Like . . . cheddar cheese and crackers!" Hailey laughed again and crammed the last cracker in her mouth.

"You think?" I couldn't suppress my smile.

Hailey nodded, her mouth too full to speak.

"Really?" I could talk about this forever. I wondered if other people thought we went together like that. Other people like Michael Lawrence, and also any other girl who might have a crush on him. My stomach did a nervous flip as I was thinking of the possibilities.

Finally, Hailey swallowed. "Really," she said, nodding her head hard.

I grinned again. "Wow."

"Are you going to ask him to dance?" said Hailey.

What?

"What do you mean?" I asked.

"At the school dance next Friday! Duh!"

"Wait, that's *next* Friday?!" I started to panic. "How can it be? Already?" I jumped up and ran to the calendar by the kitchen desk. Stabbing the Fridays with my finger, I counted ahead and there it was on November 18: *School Dance/Sam*, it said in green ink. (Green is my color on the family calendar. Allie's is blue and my mom's is red.)

My stomach got all clenchy and I had to sit down.

"Aren't you psyched?" asked Hailey. "I am!"

"No. Definitely not psyched. More like terrified! What if no one asks me to dance?"

"Oh, stop. I'm sure someone will! Probably Michael. Or what about Alex Martinez?"

"Puh-leez!" I protested. "And you'll be busy dancing with Scott the whole time and won't want to hang out with loser me." I put my head down on my arms and shook it from side to side. I imagined another headline: ***Martone a Born Wallflower.***

"Scott who?" asked Hailey, perplexed.

I looked up. "Scott *Parker*? Hello? Crush of your life? Obsession of the year?"

Hailey laughed. "Oh, *Scott*! Scott *Parker*!" She waved her hand dismissively. "I'm totally over him. He's too shy. Anyway, he had that weird stalker, and I'm just going to stay away from him and that whole scenario with a ten-foot pole!"

I had to laugh. "Okay, so who *are* you going to dance with?"

"You!" Hailey jumped up and turned on the iPod on the counter. Some horrible '80s music of my mom's came wailing out of the thing, and Hailey began doing a really funny dance, all rubbery arms with her head pumping up and down. I couldn't help laughing.

Hailey stopped. "Why are you laughing? Do I look funny dancing?"

"Wait, um . . . I thought you were just fooling around."

"No, that's my real dance," she said. "Is it bad? Do I look like a total geek?"

"Oh! Oh, no. Totally not. No. It's fine. It's . . . well, Hailey, actually . . . we have some work to do." I went over to the iPod and searched around for some music from this century. When I found a song I liked, I turned it way up loud and began to dance.

"C'mon, just copy me," I instructed.

Hailey watched me out of the corner of her eye and began trying to imitate my moves. We shook our hips from side to side and gave a little wiggle to the right, a wiggle to the left, and I pumped my bent arms at my side. Then I jumped in place to do a turn and Hailey did the same.

Hailey and I looked at each other, and I knew we were thinking the same thing: *dance lessons!*

"Where could we take dance lessons?" I asked, just as I noticed someone hovering in the doorway. It was my sister, Allie, who was filming us with her phone and laughing hysterically.

"Allie!" I screamed, and dove at her, grabbing for the phone, but she held it away from me. "Stop!" I yelled.

Hailey, meanwhile, went and switched off the music. Her face was beet red. She has two brothers and no sisters, so she worships Allie as if Allie is the high priestess of all things cool. Which she kind of is. She's pretty and funny and the star of the volleyball team. Plus, she coordinates the high school's student web site, so she's super plugged-in and has more than six hundred followers on Buddybook. *Six hundred!*

"Hey, Allie," said Hailey.

Allie turned off her phone. "You two are too much. I can't wait to post this on the school web site."

"Allie! I'm telling Mom!" I cried.

"Oh, stop. I'm just kidding," she said. "But you two could really use some dance lessons. No joke."

"We'd love dance lessons," I said. "But who would we get them from?"

Allie put her phone in her pocket and opened the fridge to stare inside. "From me, silly," said Allie. She took out some cottage cheese and carrots and sat down at the table.

Hailey and I rushed to her side and sat down. "From you?" I said. "When?"

"How about now?" asked Hailey politely, her face hopeful.

Allie looked at her watch. "Well . . ." She dipped a carrot in the cottage cheese and chewed thoughtfully.

Hailey and I glanced at each other. We were hopeful, but I was also annoyed, knowing how much Allie was enjoying the power she had over us right now.

Allie swallowed. "All right. I could do it for a little while now."

"Oh, Allie! You're the best!" cried Hailey.

I wouldn't go that far, but I was grateful. "Thanks, Al."

"Let me finish my snack and then I'll show you," she said. "Here. Plug my phone into the speakers and open up the music files."

Hailey couldn't act fast enough. She grabbed the phone, set it into the player, and scrolled through to Allie's playlist. Allie walked over and selected a song. "Okay, here's a good one," she said, and turned up the volume.

The rhythm was slow, but the chorus was kind of hypnotic. Allie began dancing in place, sway-ing from side to side, her knees bent and her arms swinging out to shoulder height in front of her. Her silver bangle bracelets jangled up and down her arm, and her hair spun out as she shook her head, looking left and right.

"See? Like this," she said. She pointed one bent knee out to the side, then the other. Left, right, left, right, left, left, right then right, right, left. All the while kind of standing in one place, with her arms moving in front of her like they were steering a car. Her head bopped to the right, then to the left. It was pretty impressive.

"And here's the coolest part, so pay attention," Allie commanded. She lifted her right hand and passed it over her head and down her back, like she was smoothing out her hair. She then did the same with her left hand. She smiled proudly. She was really good at it.

Hailey and I began trying to copy her, but it wasn't as easy as it looked. I couldn't get the rhythm down and just kept wiggling my legs till they looked (and felt) like they were made out of spaghetti. Meanwhile, Hailey kept nervously rubbing her head instead of just swiping it—she looked like she was washing her hair!

"Here, like this," said Allie. "Watch me again. Soft knees, toes pointed out about three quarters, sway left, sway right, sway left, sway right, sway left, sway right . . . now try left, left, then right, left, then right, right, right . . ."

Once she isolated the feet, I started to get it. Left, right, left . . .

But Hailey couldn't get it. Allie tried positioning Hailey's hips and arms and moving them for her, but it wasn't really working. I began incorporating the arms, one over, one under, crossing them, then doing the driving thing.

"Look! I've got it!" I cried. I danced in place for a minute, then I threw in a hair swipe of my own.

"Yay!" cried Allie, clapping. "You did get it! I never would have guessed that you'd get it before Hailey!"

I stopped dancing. "Why?"

"Well, because you're not that athletic or into moving. You're kind of a stationary person."

"So?"

"Well . . . nothing. I just didn't know you'd have such control over your limbs."

"Or that I'd have so little!" wailed Hailey. She collapsed at the kitchen table and looked up at the ceiling dramatically. "I can't daaaaaance!" she moaned.

Allie and I looked at each other and laughed. Finally, Hailey looked back at us and she was laughing too. The music was still playing.

"Somebody needs to teach *me* how to dance!" called my mom from the kitchen door, and we all *really* laughed.

"Well, we still have eleven days!" I said to Hailey. And she jumped up, and we started dancing together and laughing as the song blared on.

Chapter 3

WRITING PARTNERS GIVE EACH OTHER THE AX, PAPER SUFFERS

★ ★ ★

Michael and I met at our usual lunch table the next morning at eleven o'clock. Michael had a stack of papers with him, and our bowls of organic split pea soup with croutons cooled on our lunch trays as we looked them over.

Michael handed me a printout. "Here are the meeting minutes from the last PTA meeting. Mr. Stevenson made the original proposal then and talked about a school district in Massachusetts that had started a Pay for Play program."

I read it over and nodded.

"Then there's this one." Michael handed me another sheet, and his fingers grazed mine, sending a jolt through my whole body. I played it cool. After all, this was business. I focused on the sheet of paper in front of me. Or at least I tried to. "This is an article I got from the library about the Massachusetts plan. It's pretty tough, what they did."

I skimmed it and nodded again. I wondered if our fingers would touch again.

"And finally, there's this one. It's an op-ed piece from a paper in a nearby Massachusetts town that was considering the change as well. The writer of the opinion piece is arguing against it."

"Okay. So I can keep these?" I said.

"Yup. They're for you." Michael drew his tray in and began eating his soup. "Mmm. This soup is great!" he said, looking up at me.

We smiled at each other. Ever since we'd done a big article on how bad the cafeteria food was, the school chef had made a few changes. Now we have a homemade organic lunch item available every day, plus an optional healthy snack (like a hard-boiled egg or trail mix), but you have to pay extra for them. Some kids won't do it or maybe can't afford it. It's only an extra dollar for each, but I think it's worth it. I used to just go hungry all the time, and I am someone who does not do well with an empty stomach. The new plan was working out great for me.

I tried the soup. "You're right, this is delicious. I have to e-mail Mary and tell her!" Mary is the school chef. She's our pal now that we helped her push through the changes she wanted to make.

"So who do we need to talk to?" I asked. "I mean, besides the coaches and Mr. Pfeiffer?" Michael and I looked at each other again, and we both winced this time. Mr. Pfeiffer is the school principal, and he hasn't been a huge fan of ours ever since we did a pretty hard-hitting article on his curriculum changes a couple of issues back. I guess that's the nature of reporting: You make friends and you lose them along the way, depending on whether or not they like what you write about them.

Now Michael looked thoughtful. "I think we should try to get some quotes from coaches, students, and the school board up in Massachusetts. Just maybe as a sidebar. See how hard it is for them, why it's such a bad idea—"

"Wait. What?"

He looked at me, his bright blue eyes as clear as the sky on a sunny day and just as brilliant. "What what?"

"What do you mean it's a bad idea?" I asked. "Isn't the whole point of reporting to be objective? To find out whether it's a good idea or a bad one? We can't judge this for ourselves right from the start. We need the facts!"

Michael's beautiful eyes narrowed and grew stormy. Uh-oh. *Writing Partners Give Each Other the Ax, Paper Suffers.*

"How could it possibly be a good idea?" Michael asked.

"Why? We're in a recession," I said. (I wasn't *exactly* sure what that meant, but I heard my mom and my favorite aunt discussing it at brunch on Sunday, and I knew it meant that money was tight for a lot of people.) "Maybe we could use the money for more important things."

"What would be more important than the sports program?" asked Michael, his voice icy.

I knew he was mad, but I also thought he was wrong. "Um, hello? Lunch? Or maybe new computers? Classes that will help people find careers later in life? I mean, it's not like anyone here is going to be a professional football player. No offense."

Michael sighed. "But what about everything that sports teach too? Health, discipline, commitment, teamwork, patience . . . I could go on and on. And what if kids suddenly can't participate anymore because their families can't afford the fees? What then?" I could tell that the more he thought about it, the more upset he was getting. Angrily, he balled up his napkin and threw it down on his tray. He picked up his water glass to take a sip, and I could see that his hands were actually shaking a little. Whoa!

"Maybe you should pitch this as an opinion piece," I said quietly.

Michael was silent for a long time . . . too long.

"Hello? Earth to Mikey?" I said, trying to lighten the mood.

He sighed heavily. "Look, I care about good reporting. I care about the rules of journalism. I know we need to be impartial and present the facts so our readers can make up their own minds. It's just . . . how much more are they going to take away from us? Lots of schools have already lost art and music. I just think it has gone too far. And . . . sports are really important to me."

"I agree, and I know sports are important to you, but I'm just not sure they're an essential part of education—something the school needs to pay for."

We were quiet as we thought it over. Finally, Michael said, "Well, the good news is, we definitely have a story here. That's all Trigger wanted to know for now. Do you want to flesh it out for him or should I?"

"Maybe both of us?" I asked.

"Fine." Michael looked at my tray to see if I was finished. I was. "Let's go see him now. Ready, Pasty?" he said.

Well, he can't be too mad if he's calling me "Pasty," I thought. "Okay."

★   ★   ★

We walked down the hall to the *Voice* office.

"Well, if it isn't my two star reporters!" said Mr. Trigg, happy to see us.

We crammed into his small office off the newsroom. The walls were covered with framed front pages from British tabloids and World War II posters, plus a big photo of Winston Churchill.

"What have you two been up to?" he asked, with a twinkle in his eye.

"We've just started our digging on the afterschool sports story," explained Michael.

"And?"

I spread the pages Michael had given me out on Mr. Trigg's desk. He lifted his reading glasses from the cord around his neck and peered at the materials. "Hmm," he said, flipping through the pages. "Oh. Mmm-hmm."

Michael and I looked at each other. We couldn't tell if Mr. Trigg's noises were happy, interested noises or "go find another story" noises. Finally, he took off his glasses and looked up at us.

"Very interesting," he said. "A jolly good topic, I must say. A little hard to report at this stage, as nothing concrete has happened here, though. It's just an idea that's out there. Let's think."

We watched while he thought.

"Maybe an early story on this will encourage people to keep an eye on the topic. That way, the school board won't make a decision without everyone having a say, including the students. If we publicize the possibility, people will be watching for it and will have a chance to step in and offer their two cents when it comes up again. Journalism is all about spreading the word and making sure the reading public has all the information. I say, lead with a direct quote from Mr. Stevenson's proposal, then report on the Massachusetts story, with opinions from around here and up there, if you can get them. That should get people's attention. Righty-ho?"

I smiled. "Great."

Michael nodded.

Mr. Trigg looked from one of us to the other. "Are you both on the same page about this?"

Was the guy a mind reader or what?

We looked at each other and then back at him. "No," said Michael. "Not at all."

Mr. Trigg smiled broadly and clapped his hands. "Excellent! No better way to cover all sides of the story, then! Tea?" He plugged in his electric kettle and began gathering his tea things.

"I have class," said Michael. "Gotta go."

"Me too," I lied. "Thanks, Mr. Trigg!"

"Anytime, old chums! Cheerio!"

Michael and I left and stood uncomfortably in the hall outside the newsroom for a minute.

"Well, see you later," I said.

"Yeah. Let's . . . let's do some digging online, and then we can divvy up the calling assignments. Check in tomorrow." Michael was looking off over my shoulder. I wanted to turn around to see what he was staring at (a girl?), but it would have been a little awkward.

"Fine." Not fine! I wasn't going to see him or talk to him until tomorrow? That was an eternity!

"See ya" was all he said. And off he walked.

What? No "Pasty"? I wanted to call after him.

I never thought I'd long to hear that nickname. I hoped I hadn't ruined our relationship just by having a different opinion. I turned around to see who he'd been staring at, but it was only Frank Duane, the first-string quarterback from Michael's football team. Whew.

I pretended to walk the other way for a bit, and then when Michael was out of sight, I doubled back to the newsroom, smacking my head like I'd forgotten something, just in case anyone was watching.

"Hi, Mr. Trigg," I whispered.

"Back so soon?" he said, blowing on his hot tea. He took a sip, frowned, and then added a packet of sugar.

"I have to collect my letters." The Dear Know-It-All mailbox is in the newsroom. I closed the outside door and quickly opened up the mailbox. There were three letters. I scooped them out and buried them deep in my messenger bag. Even though Dear Know-It-All has caused me a lot of heartache, I always feel excited whenever there's a new letter to read. Like, maybe this is the one that will shoot me straight to editor in chief next year. Maybe this is the one where I'll save the day and someone will be so grateful for my advice, even though they don't know who I am.

I unlocked the door and called good-bye to Mr. Trigg. Then I set off for "earthonomics," which is what they call my merged math and science class these days, and tried not to worry about not agreeing with Michael—for the first time ever.

Chapter 4

MARTONE HAS MOVES AFTER ALL: CLASSMATES ASTOUNDED BY GRACE OF ONETIME KLUTZ!

★ ★ ★

It wasn't until after I'd finished my homework and checked all my news blogs and sites (*CNN, Huffington Post, Daily Beast, People,* and so on) that I got to my Dear Know-It-All letters. I closed my door and mentally reviewed Mr. Trigg's list of directives from when I'd first signed on as Dear Know-It-All:

- Do not reveal who you are.
- Do not reach out to the letter writer directly.

- If someone seems to be in danger in any way, notify Mr. Trigg immediately.
- Keep it wholesome.
- Be supportive and sympathetic.
- Keep it relevant. Broad subjects are better than very specific ones.
- When in doubt, talk to Mr. Trigg.
- All replies must be vetted by Mr. Trigg.
- Don't forget to make it jazzy and readable!

Individually, these were not that hard, but combined, they could make answering the letters very difficult. Like, "Keep it wholesome" and "Make it jazzy and readable" were hard to accomplish at the same time! Plus, I am a facts girl, not a natural opinion writer or advice giver. I mean, come on, I don't even know what *I'm* doing 90 percent of the time. How can I possibly give advice to anyone else on how to lead their life? Give me facts over opinions any day.

I ripped open the first envelope. It was written on Christmas stationery, which was kind of funny.

Dear Know-It-All,

I want a kitten. How can I convince my mom?

Signed,
Desperate for a Furry Friend

Hmm. That was a pretty good one. I let my mind wander over possible replies: beg; offer to do all the chores around the house and put a security deposit down so if you don't do the work you promised, then your mom keeps the money; sneak and get a kitten—once she sees its fuzzy cuteness, she won't be able to say no. There were lots of possibilities. This was a good letter. Probably the one for the next issue.

Happily, I set it aside and opened the next one. It was on lined notebook paper, in a business envelope. The handwriting was messy. It had to be written by a boy.

Dear Know-It-All,

I really want to make varsity this

year. I've been working out And
practicing A lot. WhAt else cAn I do?

From,
BAsketbAll Dude

Oh. This was also a good letter. Maybe people were finally getting the hang of what to actually ask Dear Know-It-All. This was someone I thought I could actually help with good advice. After all, I knew all about the dedication it takes to become really good at something you love. In that way, basketball was not that far off from reporting. Two good Know-It-All letters so far. Besides being interesting and unusual, these questions were very answerable.

I set the two letters aside and opened the third, knowing that just based on the odds, it would be a lousy letter. It was on pink stationery with little scallops cut along the edges. Supercute and girly, with a matching envelope. It said:

Dear Know-It-All,

I am sad. Every day at lunch, there's that yummy-looking organic food option, but my mom won't give me any extra money to buy it. She says my lunch is supposed to be included in school and that's what we pay our taxes for. What should I do so I can eat some of that good food too?

Signed,
Hungry

Oh boy. I cringed at that one. I felt responsible for the pay option, and I also felt guilty that someone couldn't get an extra five or ten dollars a week to buy decent food like I could. I wondered if the girl's mom really couldn't afford it or if she was just taking a stand on principle. I also wondered which of these three letters I would run this time. Maybe I'd save them and run each one in a row, one week after the other. Or maybe I should just pick one out of a hat. Even though each of the letters was kind of tough in its own way, it felt great to have some meaty Dear Know-It-All issues to ponder, and way before deadline, too.

To celebrate, I went back online and checked out videos of people dancing. Then I replayed one and started practicing to the music in front of my mirror. I was actually pretty good at it. I didn't look like a weirdo. Well, okay, when I did the hair-smoothing thing, I looked a little weird, but no one said I had to do that on the dance floor.

I imagined myself at the school dance, dancing away with Hailey by my side. A crowd gathers to watch us. The headline pops into my mind: ***Martone Has Moves After All: Class-mates Astounded by Grace of Onetime Klutz!*** And out of nowhere, Michael Lawrence appears and crosses the room toward me. He sweeps me into his arms—

Suddenly, there was a knock on my door. "Sam? Are you dancing?"

It was Allie, and my Know-It-All letters were still spread out all over my desk! I quickly grabbed them and shoved them under my bed, then crossed the room in two quick strides and opened the door.

Luckily, she assumed I was breathless from the dancing, but she still entered with a look of suspicion. I tell you, Allie has a better nose for news than even I do. I am sure that one day soon she will figure out that I am Dear Know-It-All. She just has that kind of brain.

She looked all around the room, and then her eyes stopped at the side of the bed. I looked and realized with a sinking sensation that there was a pink scalloped edge of stationery poking out from under the bed.

Allie looked up at me. "What's that?" she said.

I looked down, faking innocence. "Oh . . . that's . . . a love letter I'm working on, to Michael."

"Can I see it?" she asked.

"No way!" I squealed.

"Where'd you get the paper? Can I have some? It's so cute!"

Was it my imagination, or was she watching me a little too closely?

"Oh, it's Hailey's. She gave me a sheet to use."

Allie's eyebrows drew close together in suspicion. "It's pretty girly for Hailey."

I am an idiot. Everyone knows what a tomboy Hailey is. *Think, Martone, think!*

"Well . . . her grandma gave it to her last Christmas, and she's trying to get rid of it before next one."

"You can tell her she can give it to me. Or, never mind! I'll tell her myself when she comes over tomorrow!"

"How do you know she's coming over tomorrow?" I asked. Now I was the suspicious one.

"She texted me from her brother's phone to ask me for more dance lessons."

"What? My best friend is now texting you behind my back? This is an outrage!" I was pretty annoyed, but I made a bigger deal out of it so I could put Allie on the defensive. It worked.

She shrugged. "What was I supposed to say? It's not like I won't be here. Anyway, I like dancing and I think it's fun to teach other people. Don't forget, I took all those dance classes in middle school."

"Oh yeah. You were really into that. Why did you quit again?"

"They cut the program. They ran out of money. It was a major bummer. Some people continued with the teacher after she got a job at a studio downtown, but it was expensive and kind of a hassle to get there, so I never went. I haven't taken a dance class since."

"Wow. That's too bad."

"I know. I think I could have gotten pretty good. Plus, it's great exercise and the other girls were so much fun. It gave me a lot of confidence on the dance floor too."

"Yeah," I said. "Funny how a little thing like dance class could do so much for you."

"Yeah." Allie looked kind of dejected for a minute. I felt bad.

"Well, at least you had the gymnastics team," I said, reminding her what a star she'd been in middle school. She'd won medals and trophies for three years straight.

"Yeah. Too bad I didn't have the time to continue with that in high school."

"You still could!" I said encouragingly.

"Nah, it's too late. I'm out of shape."

"Hardly!" I protested.

"Well, out of training," she said.

We were quiet for a moment, thinking of the glory that might have been.

"So . . . I've been practicing my moves. I think I'm getting pretty good. Wanna see me dance?" I asked to cheer her up.

"No," she said briskly. "Just turn down the music, please." And she left.

I felt like I'd been slapped across the face. The old Allie was back. What had I been thinking, offering to dance for her like a total loser? I shut my door and rushed to my computer.

My fingers flew over the keyboard. I typed a quick IM to Hailey. If Allie brings it up, the pink scalloped stationery was a present from your grandma. Don't ask.

Then I pulled the letters back out from under the bed and tried to decide which one to answer.

Chapter 5

COLUMNIST CRACKS UNDER PRESSURE, REVEALS ALL

★ ★ ★

Last night I was up late researching the Pay to Play concept. Now my brain is more scrambled than ever! To keep everything straight, I had to get out my notebook and make a list of the pros and cons I was reading about based on stories about Pay to Play from all around the country.

CONS:
- If you have more than one child or your child plays more than one sport, the costs really add up.
- Only the well-off kids get to play the sports, and they could afford to play extracurricular club sports anywhere.

- Charging fees lowers the turnout for sports teams.

- Parents tell kids who aren't that talented to consider whether it's worth paying a fee to sit on the bench all season. (Ouch!)

PROS:

- It frees up money in the school budget for other things.

- Kids who pay to play work harder because they value their participation more.

- Teams can get corporate sponsors or hold fund-raisers, which are real community build-ers and good learning experiences for kids.

- Teams can work off the fees by doing odd jobs for the school phys ed department (mop-ping mats, inflating balls, etc.).

- Payment plans and scholarships are available.

My head was spinning from all of this. I could see a little more clearly now why Michael was against it. We do have a lot of less fortunate kids at our school, and this would be hard on them. If they couldn't come up with the money, it would be difficult for them to participate. On the other hand, why should the taxpayers' money go to sports that not every child participates in?

I ran into Michael in the hall this morning near my locker. He wasn't as smiley as usual, which made my stomach flutter nervously. Was he mad at me? I wanted to ask, but I didn't dare.

"Uh, I just wanted to let you know that I did a bunch of research online last night for our article. I made a list. We could go over it at lunch?" I cringed, suddenly feeling like I was asking him out and unsure of whether he'd say yes.

"Okay, Listy. That's fine. I'll see you there." And he strode off down the hall. "Hey, Frank!" I heard him call.

Okay. Whatever. Distracted much?

"Sammy! Whazzup?"

It was Hailey.

"I do *not* know what's up, Hailey. I *really* don't know," I said, shaking my head.

"Love problems?" she asked, looking down

the hall at Michael, who was in heated conversation with his teammate.

I sighed. "I guess. Something is up with him, but I can't figure it out. I can't tell if he's mad at me for disagreeing with him about the Pay to Play thing or if he's just distracted."

"Hey, maybe you should write to Dear Know-It-All. She'll help you!" I looked at Hailey suspiciously. Did she know? But she was simply unloading her backpack into her locker. No, she didn't know. But how I wished I could tell her, right then and there. Ugh! Keeping a big secret from your best friend is torture. *Columnist Cracks Under Pressure, Reveals All.* Hailey slammed her locker and zipped her backpack.

"Lunch plans later?"

"I'm meeting Michael to go over facts for our article. You can join us." I didn't sound that enthusiastic, though, and she got the message.

"Nah. Don't want to intrude on a lovers' quarrel. But come to my soccer practice and then we can walk home to your house afterward. Allie said she'll work on my dance moves." Then Hailey busted a couple of moves right there in the hallway, but they were so bad, I reached out and stopped her before anyone saw.

"Hailey. Don't. Just don't. You are not ready for your public yet," I said. "And by the way, don't text my sister."

"Why?" asked Hailey innocently. But I knew she knew the answer.

"Because it flatters her and annoys me, and if even *one* of those reasons isn't good enough, then you're not my best friend anymore."

"Oh, fine. I don't have time to find a new best friend today anyway," said Hailey, all fake irritated. But then she laughed and slapped me on the back with her earthonomics notebook, and we were off.

★　　★　　★

Michael didn't come to lunch.

I got my tray and looked for him. He always beats me and saves me a spot at our usual table, but today he just wasn't there. I decided to go to an empty table that I didn't usually sit at, kind of in Siberia, figuring if I went and sat with my girl-friends, he'd never want to join me when he finally did show up. But he didn't. Show up, that is.

I ate my veggie wrap, visited my kitchen friend Carmen, who was selling wasabi peas as a snack, bought some, told her they were gross, laughed, got my money back, and went to say hi to Hailey, who was sitting with two of our other friends, Tricia and Meg. And still no Michael! By the end of lunch period, I was mad.

For the early part of the afternoon, I fumed. For the later part, I was hurt. When Hailey's soccer practice rolled around, I was worried. I still hadn't seen Michael. Why won't my mom let me have my own phone?! (*Because it's too expensive, that's why!* I could hear her saying.)

But as I crossed the field to the bleachers to watch Hailey, I saw him warming up with the rest of the football team. Now I was mad again. I had expected him to be sick and to have gone home (most likely). Or to have been blown up in the science lab by some experiment gone wrong (less likely). Or maybe in detention for doing something bad (unlikely). But to see him there, perfectly fine and fit as a fiddle, meant that he had either forgotten about our plan (bad) or blown me off (worse).

I sat there, trying to focus on getting some homework done and occasionally watching Hailey, but my eyes kept getting drawn back to Michael Lawrence, in his football pants and gigantic shoulder pads. He looked hotter and hunkier than ever, which was annoying. I wondered if he saw me, because if he did, he didn't show it.

Hailey was now doing the drill that she was known for: ball juggling. This is when you try to see how many times you can bounce a soccer ball off your head, knee, foot, chest, or anywhere but your hands, all without letting it touch the ground. Hailey can do it about a hundred times. I can do it *twice*, just to put things in perspective. (The only sport I'm any good at is gymnastics—specifically, the uneven parallel bars—and I think that's only because I can't trip while I'm doing it!)

Hailey is so coordinated and graceful on the soccer team that it's funny she can't make her body do what she wants when she's trying to dance. You would think she'd be amazing. I counted seventy-five juggles before the ball fell, and when it did, I cheered and clapped. I couldn't help myself. It was that impressive. Hailey took a bow and her teammates laughed at us.

I glanced over, and Michael was definitely looking in my direction to find out what the commotion was. He had seen me. He raised his hand in a wave and I turned away. Like I'd be caught looking at him across a field! Like I'd wave at someone who'd stood me up for lunch. Humph!

Hailey's practice ended before the football team's, so we were able to leave without having to speak to Michael. But I was grumpier now than I'd been all day, and poor Hailey couldn't cheer me out of it.

"You know, Sammy, you should play soccer with me. Just think—you'd get to see Michael in those tight pants every day. It's really good exercise, and it helps control stress, which I can see you have a lot of, and who knows, maybe you'd be great! You've got those long legs. I bet you can still run really fast."

"Hailey, I won one race in first grade because six kids were out with the flu. You've got to get it through your head once and for all that I'm not fast!" I said. "And I'm not competitive."

"Sure you are!" said Hailey. "Maybe not with sports, but what about all those board games you love?"

"Well, that has nothing to do with sports, and I am *not* trying out for soccer. I have enough on my plate to worry about without adding anything else." Uh-oh. I was heading into Dear Know-It-All territory. All Hailey had to do was ask about what else I had on my plate and I'd be in big trouble! Quickly, I redirected the conversation. "By the way, have you ever heard of paying to play on sports teams at school? Cherry Valley is thinking about starting that."

"Really? Huh." Hailey thought for a minute, which was not the reaction I was expecting.

"Wouldn't you be furious?" I prompted.

But Hailey wasn't upset at all. "I don't know." She shrugged. "My cousins do that in Pennsylvania. Actually, they were surprised that we don't have to pay anything for our teams. They thought everyone had to pay something for school teams."

"So they don't mind?"

"No, but they're used to it, I guess. And they have fund-raisers for their teams that are really fun. They have car washes and bake sales and they sell candy and wrapping paper and stuff like that. It's kind of fun because they all do it together. Oh, they also get stores in their town to sponsor them, and then they put the stores' names on their jerseys."

"That's terrible! It's like selling out!" I said. I was horrified by the idea of selling advertising on your clothing to the highest bidder. It was one topic I had looked forward to agreeing on with Michael today before he blew me off.

But Hailey felt the opposite. "No way! They love it! It makes them feel like professionals, being sponsored. They think it's really cool. Plus, then they get more fans, because the businesses advertise to tell their customers when the games are and stuff."

"Oh. That does sound kind of cool. Hang on."
I whipped out my notebook and jotted down a few
things on my Pay to Play pros list. "Anything else
to add?" I asked, my pen poised.

"Well, I'm not sure if you know this part
already, but the coaches are always saying that
the school budget doesn't come close to covering the costs of the program. They get grants and
donations already, just to keep things going."

I scribbled that down too and wrote *Research
this* in the margin next to it. "Thanks," I said. I
clicked my pen closed and we walked on.

"Yeah, I guess I wouldn't really mind," said
Hailey.

"Yeah, but would your parents?" I asked.

"I don't know. I'll ask them tonight," Hailey
said, "and I'll get back to you."

★　　★　　★

At my house, we had a snack and started Hailey's
homework while we waited for Allie. I was midbite
into a microwaved s'more when the phone rang. I
chewed quickly as I crossed the room to get it.

LAWRENCE, THOMAS said the caller ID. Michael's dad's name.

My hand flew to my mouth. "It's him!" I yelled through a mouthful of crumbs. "Do I get it or not?"

"Get it, you idiot!" said Hailey.

It was the fourth ring. It was about to go to voice mail. Chew, chew, gulp.

"Hello?" I said.

"Hi, is Sam there, please? It's Michael Lawrence." His voice sounded deep on the phone, and my legs turned to jelly.

Quickly, I considered pretending to be someone else and taking a message. Then I considered being frosty. But instead, I decided not to play games. "Sam can't come to the phone right now because you're a ditcher," I joked.

"I thought it was you. I am so sorry. I really am. I had a major team crisis and I . . . I just lost track of time. Listen, could I . . . could I come over?" he asked.

My eyes flew open wide. I looked at Hailey. "Right now? Here?" I said. Hailey nodded emphatically, grinned, and quietly clapped her hands.

I pointed at her like, *What about you?* But she waved me off.

"Um, okay. Fine. Come on by," I said. I worried for a moment because my mom wasn't home, but it wasn't like I was going to be alone with Michael. Hailey was here, and Allie was due home from school any minute now.

"Thanks. I'll be right over." Was it just me, or did he sound relieved?

I hung up. "Sorry," I said to Hailey. "I didn't know what else to say. Let me just call my mom for a second." I quickly called my mom at work just to let her know Michael was dropping by. Then I turned back to Hailey. "Are you sure you're okay with this?" I said. "You're really not mad?"

"Oh, please, don't worry about me. It's not like it's every day that the crush of your dreams calls you and asks if he can come over, right?"

I stared dreamily into space.

"Right? Um, Earth to Sam, that was a question."

"Oh, huh? Yeah. Right. Not every day. That's for sure!" For the moment, I wasn't mad at Michael anymore. And depending on what he had to say when he got here, I might not be mad at him then, either.

"Are you gonna ask him to dance next Friday?" asked Hailey for what felt like the millionth time.

"Ugh. I don't know! I'm sure everyone will just dance in a big group or something, right?"

"I don't know!" Hailey said in a singsong voice.

The front door opened and closed. "Hello! Hailey? Sam?"

It was Allie.

"Hey. We're in the kitchen, just chilling," Hailey called back, trying to sound cool. These two were torture! I didn't know if I could stick it out with them for a whole dance lesson.

Wait! The dance lesson! And Michael!

"Allie!" I called urgently. "We have a situation! Quick!"

Allie didn't reply. Texting as usual. Why couldn't she finish her texting before she walked in the door, that's what I wanted to know. Why did she always have to walk in and then stand there, unavailable?

"Thanks for the rapid response," I called tartly.

Silence. She was still texting.

I rolled my eyes at Hailey. She shook her head sadly. "You just don't understand what it's like to be in high school," Hailey said, all condescending.

"Oh, shut up," I said. "Neither do you!"

Allie finally entered the kitchen.

"Allie, Michael Lawrence is coming over. As in *right now*!" I said dramatically.

Allie crossed the room, cool as a cucumber, and I hated her for it. She even had a small, smug smile on her face. "Really?" she said. "What perfect timing. I can teach him how to dance too!"

"Oh no! No way! NO WAY!! You two are not to breathe one word of these dance lessons to him. For both our sakes. Hailey, please!" I jumped out of my chair and began waving my arms around.

But Hailey was quite thrilled to be Allie's coconspirator. They smiled patiently at me as I freaked out.

"Guys, please! Do *not* let him know I'm trying to learn how to dance. He'll think I am such a loser! Please!" I hid my face in my hands.

"Maybe we will and maybe we won't," said

Allie, winking at Hailey. "What's it worth to ya?"

"Yeah, I don't even care if he finds out I'm getting dance lessons. Doesn't make any difference to me!" said Hailey. I wanted to choke her right then and there, but the doorbell rang. I pointed my finger at both of them and stared them viciously in the eyes as I backed out of the kitchen. Then I drew my finger across my throat like a sword. "Not a word, or else!" I said.

"Oh, we are *shaking*!" said Allie.

"Petrified," agreed Hailey, and then they both cackled.

I was the one who was both shaking and petrified, however.

Chapter 6

MARTONE GETS CHANCE TO COMFORT PARTNER! IS ROMANCE IN THE AIR?

★ ★ ★

"Hello, *Mikey*," I said, opening the door wide.

"Hey, Paste. I'm sorry about earlier, about missing lunch. Really, I—" He reached behind his back and brought out a Tupperware container. "Here," he said, stretching his hand out to me. "I brought you these to make up for it."

"Well, thanks, I guess," I said. "Leftovers?" I looked into the clear plastic container from the side.

"Not leftovers. Cinnamon buns. I made them last night." Michael Lawrence makes the best cinnamon buns in the world. They're his specialty.

Gorgeous *and* he can cook! My irritation melted. "Thanks!" I said. "Come on in."

I led him to the kitchen. "Hailey's here," I said as we walked up.

"Hey, Lawrence," said Hailey, all jocky cool.

"Hi, Michael!" said Allie. "Long time no see." She smirked at me. Annoying!

"Hi. I'm sorry. I hope I'm not interrupting," he said.

I stared daggers at Allie and Hailey. They'd better not even say the word "dance," or I would physically attack them. They looked at me, then they looked at Michael.

"Actually, I'm just here for some tutoring help," said Hailey. I sighed in relief.

"Yeah, we'll get going and leave you two . . . alone," said Allie. I knew she wanted to say "lovebirds," but she knew I'd tell Mom and she'd get in major trouble.

"Hey, Hailey, do you have any more of that pink stationery your grandma gave you?" asked Allie as they left the room.

I gritted my teeth and fake smiled at Michael.

"Why don't you sit down?" I asked, gesturing awkwardly at the table. "Would you like something to drink?"

"Sure. Thanks. I'll just have some water, please. I can get it," he said.

"I've got it. So what's up?" I asked, turning away and trying to be all cool, as though the crush of my life sat in my kitchen every day. I wasn't going to mention lunch again. I filled a water glass, but when I turned back to the table, Michael was looking forlornly down at his sneakers. "Michael, are you all right?" I walked over to where he was sitting and squatted next to him so I could look up at his face. It was like a scene out of a movie. ***Martone Gets Chance to Comfort Partner! Is Romance in the Air?***

Michael looked back up. "Yeah. Sorry. I just . . . Thanks." He reached for the glass of water and took a big, long sip. I stared at him in concern. He put the glass down and looked at me. "You know Frank Duane? The star on our team? First-string quarterback?" I nodded. "His parents both lost their jobs in the past week, and with five kids, they're really in a tight spot. Frank is looking for an after-school job, and he's probably going to have to quit the team to do it."

I sat down. "That's terrible. Sorry to hear that."

"I know. It's tough on him, on the whole family, and with the holidays coming up so soon . . . But it really stinks for the football team. We were doing so well, mostly thanks to Frank."

"Bummer."

Michael nodded. "Anyway, today we had a last-minute meeting with the coach at lunchtime, and it ran late, and I just couldn't get back in to tell you why I wasn't there. I'm so sorry."

"That's all right," I said. He really did look sorry. We sat at the table in silence for a minute, and I suddenly realized I could hear music and thumping from Allie's room upstairs.

Michael started to laugh. "Are they *dancing* up there?" he asked. I nodded, not sure exactly what he thought of it.

"That's funny," he said, shaking his head. "What subject would assign dancing for homework?"

"Music appreciation?" I said, trying to make a little joke. Mentally, I reminded myself to kill Allie and Hailey later.

"So when will Frank know for sure if he needs to quit the team?" I asked.

Michael shook his head. "I don't know. But by the way, all the Duane kids play three sports in school," he added, nodding at me. "They're all superathletic. That's also what I've been talking with Frank about."

"What?" I asked.

"I asked if he'd be willing to be interviewed for our article. And also if he'd be willing to speak at the next PTA meeting against Pay to Play, if it comes to that."

I nodded. *Frank would be a good face to put on the cause*, I thought. I wondered how I could make a case for Pay for Play if it would be so hard for a family like Frank's. I bit my lower lip.

"Anyway, I'm sorry about today," Michael said. "I'll make it up to you. Let's meet tomorrow at lunch instead, okay? But we've really got to hustle after that because it's already Wednesday.

With the paper coming out every other Friday, we'll have to start writing by Monday at the latest. It doesn't leave us a lot of time."

"Let me know if you think there's anything I can do to help Frank," I said. "And good luck with the team and everything." I'm obviously not a sports fan, but needless to say, I *am* a Michael Lawrence fan, and I hated to see him stressed out and down in the dumps. He nodded solemnly and stood up, pushing in his chair.

"Thanks for the water," he said, depositing the glass in the sink.

I walked him to the door. "Thanks for the cinnamon buns," I said, suddenly feeling a little awkward.

And that was when Michael turned around and gave me a hug that was so quick, it was over before I realized it was happening.

"And thanks for understanding, Pasty," he said, and he hurried away.

I fainted right there in the doorway.

Just kidding. But I almost did. I began climbing the stairs to find Hailey, but my thoughts were clouded with images of Michael Lawrence hugging me. Upstairs, the music was much louder. I opened the door to Allie's room, and Hailey was dancing—some crazy dance I'd never seen before. Allie was observing Hailey from the beanbag chair next to the iPod dock. I stood there and watched as Hailey went nuts to the music with her eyes closed. And you know what? She wasn't half bad.

She definitely was dancing, in her own kooky, ball-juggling kind of way. One knee up, the other knee up, head thrown forward, shoulder rolled back . . . It looked like fun. I couldn't help myself; I jumped in and started trying to do the same moves.

But suddenly, the music stopped, "Whoa, whoa, whoa—stop right there, missy!" Hailey and I froze, like we'd been awakened from a dream. We didn't know who Allie meant.

Hailey pointed at herself with a cocked thumb. "Me?" she said.

Allie shook her head sadly. "No. My sister Spaghetti Legs over there. Sam, you look like a

Muppet that just chugged three espressos! What on Earth are you doing?"

Hailey giggled.

"I'm . . . doing the juggle, like Hailey."

"Well, you can't. So don't," said Allie, and she turned the music back up. Hailey began dancing again, and I sat morosely on the side of Allie's bed and watched. When the song was over, Hailey stood panting.

"So, have I got moves?" she asked.

Allie, mean old witch that she is, didn't answer right away. She tilted her head to the side as if really weighing her answer and finally said, "Yes."

"Really?" Hailey squealed and jumped up and down, clapping like she'd just won a TV dancing competition. I rolled my eyes, annoyed at her for being thrilled by a tiny crumb of praise from such an obnoxious source. I mean, who really cared what Allie thought anyway? Allie nodded. "Yup. I think you'll be fine. Just make sure to wear something . . . feminine."

"Feminine? You mean like a skirt?" Hailey looked horrified. You would have thought Allie told her to put on false eyelashes and red lipstick. She is a total tomboy.

"It doesn't have to be a skirt, but maybe something on top that's flowy or flowered. Do you have something like that?"

Hailey most certainly did not, but she nodded. "I'll check."

I raised my eyebrows at her and Hailey shrugged at me, irritated. "What?" she said.

"Whatever. Let's go, J.Lo," I said.

"Thank you so, sooooo much, Allie. I will never forget this!" said Hailey.

Allie waved modestly, like Queen Elizabeth. "It was no problem. You did it all yourself."

"No! It was all you!" protested Hailey.

I pulled Hailey away from her idol. I was ready to puke.

"Bye!"

Once we were inside my room, I closed the door and explained everything Michael had told me about Frank Duane. I didn't mention the hug. I don't know exactly why. I just wanted to keep it to myself. It seemed more special that way.

"Well, I'm glad Michael didn't ditch you for no reason today, but I don't like the reason he ditched you," said Hailey. She more than anyone would sympathize with an athlete who might be forced to a quit a team. Hailey looked at her reflection in my bedroom mirror and fluffed her hair.

"I'd be happy to help out a family in need, but I don't think the sports fees are the main issue," she continued.

"What do you mean?" I asked. I was surprised to hear her say that.

"Well, I bet the school would cut them a break or something, at least at first. If they need a food drive or some funding from a bake sale or something, we could do that. But right now I'm the one who needs help! Let's finish this homework so I can get home in time for dinner."

"Stir-fried tofu again?" I teased. Hailey's mom is a health-food nut.

"Probably." Hailey sighed. "But you know what? I'm so hungry after all that dancing, even tofu sounds pretty good." We both laughed as we dove into Hailey's language arts book.

Chapter 7

JOURNO'S NOSE FOR NEWS FAILS HER!

★ ★ ★

Later that night Hailey called me. She rarely calls me, preferring to IM or e-mail, so I was surprised when my mom yelled up the stairs to me after the phone rang. "Hey," I said. "What's up?" As usual, Hailey cut to the chase, as if we'd just been speaking seconds ago.

"My parents and I were talking at dinner about all the Pay to Play stuff and the Duanes and everything, and my mom said this rang a bell. She still gets the PTA minutes and agendas and everything from when she was really involved a couple of years ago, remember?"

"Of course, how could I forget?" Hailey's insider knowledge of the PTA saved my butt a couple of issues back, when I needed proof of something from a PTA meeting and she knew exactly where to find it.

"Anyway, after dinner she went to her desk to sift through her e-mails and she found what she was looking for. It sounds like the Pay to Play thing might really happen. Soon. It's scheduled for a vote at Monday night's meeting."

"What?!" I couldn't believe my ears. How had I not heard about this? ***Journo's Nose for News Fails Her!***

"Yeah," said Hailey with a sigh. "And by the way, my parents are for it."

"Well, I'm for it too. Or I was, until I heard about the Duanes. Now I'm not sure what to think," I said. We were quiet for a moment. "I guess I'd better call Michael," I said.

"You go, girl," said Hailey.

"He will *not* be psyched," I predicted. "And, Hails, thanks."

"No prob," said Hailey, pleased with her use-fulness. "Bye."

I hung up the phone and went to look up Michael's number in the phone book.

Ha! Just kidding! Of course I know it by heart, even though I've only used it like once or twice. I dialed, and someone with a deep voice answered (his dad? a brother?).

"Hi, is Michael there, please?" I asked.

"Sure, just a minute," said the voice. "Who's calling?"

"It's . . ." I hesitated. "Sam" sounded so boyish and boring. Impulsively, I said, "Samantha."

"Okay. Hang on." Then I heard the voice yelling, "Mikeyyy! Samaaantha calling!" The voice was kind of teasing. Definitely a brother. I blushed up to the roots of my hair. If I'd been walking, I would have tripped. I tried to take deep breaths to calm myself.

"Hello?" said Michael, his voice peppy and maybe even a little breathless, too.

"Hi. It's Sam," I said.

"Oh." Michael laughed. "You threw me for a loop with 'Samantha'! You should have just said it was Pasty."

"Very funny," I said. I heard a receiver jostling.

"Hang up, Will!" yelled Michael. I thought I heard laughter as the receiver clanked into its base.

"Sorry. Those guys are torture," said Michael, irritated now. "What's up?" He had sounded so happy when he first answered the phone that I hated to burst his bubble.

"I have some news," I said. "The PTA is voting on Pay to Play on Monday night. They're not really publicizing it, so it makes me think they don't want any debate. What do you want to do?"

Michael whistled. "Sneaky. Where did you hear this?"

I hesitated. Hailey had had a little crush on Michael not that long ago, and when I found out, I'd wondered if he secretly liked her, too. "Hailey," I said finally. "Her mom still gets the PTA executive board e-mails."

"Wow," said Michael. "So it's definitely true, then."

I bristled. "I told you it was true. Don't you trust me?"

"Sorry. I mean, I'm just thinking out loud. Of course I trust you."

"Humph," I said. "So what should we do?"

Michael was quiet.

"Hello?" I said after a few seconds.

"I'm thinking," he replied. "You know what? I need to really think this one through. Can I sleep on it, and we'll meet by your locker in the morning to make our plan?"

"Sure. What time?"

"Eight ten," he said. "See you then."

I hung up and double-checked that the phone was off. Then I gave a big whoop of post–nervous energy, crush-calling nerdiness and sort of danced back to my room to finish my homework. Thank goodness no one saw me. (And by "no one," I think we all know I mean Allie.) Back at my desk, I tried to picture myself dancing in the darkened school gymnasium with Michael, but somehow my imagination failed me. Would I ask him to dance? Would he ask me? Would I trip over my own two feet as soon as I hit the dance floor? I sighed and decided to Google the Pay for Play thing some more. Anything to stay online and check out news sites.

★ ★ ★

The next morning Michael was at my locker when I arrived. What a great feeling to have the cutest guy at school standing there waiting for me first thing! But he was not happy. "Frank got a job drying cars at his uncle's car wash. He's off the team for now," he said.

"Oh no!"

Michael looked angry. "And if Pay for Play goes through, we're going to lose other valuable players. We really need to organize a protest. Maybe a sit-in. Like Occupy Cherry Valley, I'm thinking."

"Wow. Really?" I said. *But what if I'm not sure I'm against it?* I thought.

Michael nodded firmly.

"So . . . everyone you've discussed this with is against it?" I asked.

"Yes," said Michael confidently.

But what about your own writing partner? I wanted to ask. "Have you done a survey online?" I asked. Michael had done that once before, and it was very successful.

"Not yet, but I'm putting one up on Buddybook

tonight. I'll present the results at the PTA meeting on Monday."

Michael was so riled up, I had to wonder if he'd be able to report any of this objectively. In fact, I knew he couldn't, but I wasn't sure what to say. I didn't want to make him mad. Or madder than he already was. Or anyway, mad at me!

"Okay...," I said hesitantly. "So what should I do?"

"For one thing, spread the word about the meeting and try to get as many people as possible to go. Maybe your sister could mention it on Buddybook or something."

I cringed. I hated getting Allie involved with anything, but if Michael was doing the asking . . . it was hard to say no.

"And let's go to the newsroom at lunchtime and create a flyer to hand out that invites people and their parents to the PTA meeting on Monday," he added. "Tell them to search for 'Pay for Play' online." Michael looked up at the ceiling as he brainstormed.

I thought about everything Michael was asking me to do. Letting people know about a meeting was a good use of our reporting and news resources. So as long as we just did that, we weren't taking any sides. We were just reporting the news, like any good journalist would. I was just nervous to get into sit-ins and things like that. That didn't sound very objective to me.

"I'll spread the word that we need to be ready to stage a protest if the vote doesn't go our way on Monday," Michael said.

"Are you going to put that in writing?" I asked. I was alarmed by that idea.

"No, of course not." Michael looked at me like I was an idiot, which I did not like.

"Sorry, just checking. Sheesh." Inside, I was really torn. I wanted to tell him I still wasn't sure I was on his side, but I wanted him to like me. I didn't know what to do, and I was starting to feel really stressed out.

"All right, I've got to run to class. Don't forget: newsroom at eleven, okay, Pasty? Later." And off he ran.

I sighed, hoisted my messenger bag over my shoulder, and trudged off to language arts.

Chapter 8

JOURNO CONVINCES TRUE LOVE HE'S WRONG

★ ★ ★

All through my morning classes, I stressed.

I stressed about Michael and how he'd hate me if he found out I wasn't really against the Pay for Play idea.

I stressed about how Michael was getting overly involved in this story. Journalists weren't supposed to get personally involved!

I stressed about Frank Duane and his family.

And I stressed about the school dance.

I even stressed about my Dear Know-It-All column. Which question would I run this week? I couldn't decide. There was only one thing to do and that was to go see Mr. Trigg. But how could I talk to him without seeming like I was ratting out Michael? *That* was stressing me out more than anything.

★   ★   ★

When I got out of class at 10:45, I was right by the newsroom. I crossed my fingers that Trigger would be there and that he'd be alone, and I was in luck.

"Knock, knock! Hi, Mr. Trigg!" I called.

"Ms. Martone! How lovely to see you!" he replied, pushing back from his desk so he could see me through the doorway of his small office. "How's the news business?"

I crossed the room quickly. "Not so great, Mr. Trigg," I confessed quietly, checking over my shoulder to make sure no one had followed me into the newsroom.

Mr. Trigg's face was concerned. "Is everything all right? Are you in trouble again?" Earlier this year, I had been cyberbullied by a girl who didn't like the advice I gave her in my Dear Know-It-All column. Mr. Trigg felt terrible because he had been away when the cyberbullying started. Anyway, I had to reassure him that what I was upset about now wasn't like that.

"No, nothing bad or dangerous. Thanks. I just . . ." I didn't know where to begin. "I . . ."

The newsroom door opened and it was Michael. "Hey, Sam! Hey, Mr. Trigg!" he called out enthusiastically. He was all fired up still and raring to go. He crossed the room to where I stood, leaning in Mr. Trigg's doorway.

"What's up?" he asked, seeing the serious looks on our faces.

"Hello, Mr. Lawrence," said Trigger. "How are things with you?" I noticed Mr. Trigg eyeing Michael carefully.

"Well, terrible and great. The terrible part is that the PTA is looking to move ahead on the Pay to Play idea. They're voting on it this Monday. The other terrible part is the football team has lost its star player because his family needs money, and he had to quit the team and get a job. The great part is, we have a plan to fight Pay to Play, right, Sammy?" He nudged me.

I smiled weakly. "Right," I said. Trigger looked

back and forth between us, trying to puzzle out what was going on beneath the surface. I wished I could have pushed a pause button on Michael's arrival and explained everything to Trigger first. Who knew when I'd have the chance again?

"So Sam and I are going to make up some flyers here. We won't be in your way, will we?" asked Michael.

"Flyers about what?" asked Mr. Trigg.

"Telling kids to come to the PTA meeting on Monday and bring their parents, so we can fight this thing!" Michael ditched his book bag and sat down at a computer and began typing furiously. Mr. Trigg and I looked at each other, and I knew then that he sensed my lack of enthusiasm. He nodded slowly, then folded his arms and cupped his chin while he thought for a moment.

"Sam! What are you waiting for? Come on!" called Michael.

"Ms. Martone was actually just about to run a quick errand with me," replied Mr. Trigg. "Are you ready, Ms. Martone?" He stood up and grabbed the long green-and-blue-striped wool scarf that he always wore when he left the office (even just to go to the cafeteria). I guess it was his trademark.

Feeling weak in the knees with relief, I caught right on. "All set. Let's do it!" I replied cheerily. "Be right back, Michael!" I chirped, and I followed Mr. Trigg out of the office.

Michael was so engrossed in his flyer that he just waved absentmindedly at us as we left. A clean getaway! Out in the hall, Mr. Trigg strode ahead until we reached an empty classroom and he ducked inside, flipping on the lights, closing the door behind him, and sitting down at the desk farthest from the door.

"What gives, Martone?" he asked. I smiled, knowing how he loves mysteries. This hiding out for a private conversation was right up his alley. I decided to start small.

"A couple of things. For one . . . I have three Dear Know-It-All letters I like, and I can't decide which one to print."

"Hmm. Would all three make interesting columns?" he asked.

I nodded. "Yup. They're all good."

Mr. Trigg cupped his chin again. "My first instinct is to say run one and hold two for later use. But on the other hand, I hate stale news. What if . . . what if we run a 'harvest bounty' issue and do all three, each a little shorter than usual?" he suggested with a smile.

"Harvest bounty? Oh, wait, you mean like a bonus of Dear Know-It-Alls?" I asked, getting the concept.

Mr. Trigg clapped. "Excellent! Yes! A three-for-one sale! Could you do it? It's not too much work?" His bushy gray eyebrows drew together in concern.

"No. It'll be fun. I can do it. It'll be good to change it up, anyway, keep it fresh."

Mr. Trigg beamed. "Listen to one of my protégés! Music to my ears! News is all about being fresh!"

"Okay, now for the harder stuff. I'm not sure how to say this . . ."

"Just shoot," said Mr. Trigg. "I'm all ears."

"Well . . ." I tried to choose my words carefully. "It's just . . . Michael and I don't see eye to eye on the Pay to Play issue," I said finally.

"I sensed that," said Mr. Trigg. "Your enthusiasm is not as great as his."

"It's not that I'm not enthusiastic," I said. "It's
just, he's against it and, well, I'm kind of for it. I
thought we could approach it from two sides and
write an objective article, but it's not quite shap-
ing up that way. Michael hates the idea of Pay for
Play. I'm afraid any article we write about it is
going to be completely slanted against it."

"Interesting. And why is he against it?" asked
Mr. Trigg.

"I think mostly because he plays sports and
because now he has a teammate who had to quit
because of money problems at home, and he
thinks there will be more kids like him."

Mr. Trigg nodded. "Mmm-hmm. And you?"

"I'm for it because, well, I'm not an athlete,
for one. And I think tax dollars should be used on
things that help everyone, not just stuff that some
people do."

Mr. Trigg nodded again. I couldn't tell which
side he was on. Of course, he was the poster boy

for objective news reporting. He was quiet for a moment, thinking. "It sounds like we need three articles, all on one page," he said finally. "One— maybe even a small box—that explains the issue objectively. Then maybe two opinion articles? One for it and one against it?"

My journalist senses tingled. That would be a great feature. I could already map out in my head what I'd say. I felt I had a pretty strong case. But could I really go head–to–head with Michael like that? My writing partner? My future co–editor in chief, I hoped? My future . . . boyfriend, maybe? Or at the very least, my dance partner for next Friday?

"Well, Ms. Martone? What do you say?"

I took a deep breath. "As a journalist, I love it. As a . . . friend, I'm not so sure," I confessed.

Mr. Trigg looked disappointed. "I guess it would be quite awkward for you and Michael, wouldn't it?"

I nodded sadly. "And I'm not sure I can risk that right now," I admitted.

"I can see that would be difficult. But maybe

by each of you stating your case, you can meet in the middle and find parts of each of your arguments that you agree with?"

Journo Convinces True Love He's Wrong.

"I'm sure Michael and I can write an objective article," I say slowly. "And I think he'd really like writing the opinion piece. But I'm not so sure I want to write one too."

"Well, I'll leave that up to you." Mr. Trigg smiled at me. "You have until the deadline to change your mind, and I'll speak to Mr. Lawrence about the opinion piece." He stood up and started to leave the classroom.

"Wait! Mr. Trigg! What was our errand?" I asked urgently.

"Right! Uh . . ." He cast a look around the classroom, and then, spying a dictionary, snatched it up. "This! I couldn't find the newsroom dictionary and you were showing me where I could borrow one!"

I grinned. "Lying and stealing. You've got to love journalism!"

Mr. Trigg smiled. "I'll bring it back. Anyway,

it's all in the name of truth, right?"

"Right," I agreed, and I ran off to help Michael make the flyers. I didn't disagree with inviting people to the PTA meeting. I could still do that! Maybe everything was going to work out after all.

Chapter 9

WOODWARD AND BERNSTEIN, TORN APART BY WORK

★ ★ ★

Half an hour later, Michael and I stood at the door to the cafeteria, handing out the flyers.

COME ONE, COME ALL!

Cherry Valley Middle School
Parent-Teacher Association meeting
Monday, November 14, at 6:00 p.m.
Cherry Valley Middle School Auditorium

Pay for Play debate!
Google "Pay for Play" for more information!
Let the administration know how you feel!

* Take our survey tonight on
Buddybook!*
Please give this flyer to your parents!

I convinced Michael to make it as objective as possible in the name of journalism. He reluctantly agreed. But so many kids are taking flyers that Michael was pumped, feeling like he was really doing something good for the community, while I felt like a worm, knowing I'd betray him in the press next week.

I handed out my stack as quickly as possible, just trying to get through it, and when Michael offered me some of his stack to hand out, I turned him down, saying I was starving. He knows how hungry I get, so he didn't protest, and I was so relieved to be done that I rushed through the line and ran to join Hailey, forgetting even to save a seat for Michael. Whoops. A few minutes later, he came to join us and there were no free seats at the table. He still had a stack of flyers in his hand. He must've gotten hungry too. His tray had a bowl of homemade organic chicken noodle soup on it from the premium table.

I stood up. "Hey, hand me the soup and you can ditch your tray. Then we'll drag up an extra chair and you can wedge in here." But Michael wasn't interested. He even seemed a little annoyed.

"No, that's fine. I'll go sit with Jeff." Jeff Perry is the newspaper's photographer and one of Michael's best friends. I felt terrible.

"I'm sorry. I didn't know you'd be done so fast. I thought these people would all be gone by the time—"

Michael shook his head. "Don't worry about it. It's fine." He turned and walked away. I turned and looked at Hailey.

"Whoops," she said.

"Big whoops," I agreed. "Why am I such an idiot?"

"You're not an idiot," she said. "But you kind of are, actually. Not about saving the seat, but about handing out the flyers. Listen, Pay to Play is happening, Sam. It can't not. The school district has to cut something, and it's not going to be language farts, unfortunately."

I rolled my eyes. "I know, Hailey. I don't really care either way since I'm not on any sports team anyway."

"Wait, you're not?" joked Hailey.

"Very funny. Anyway, I was just trying to be supportive of Michael," I said. "So much for that, now that he hates me."

"Love is too time-consuming for me," said Hailey breezily. "It's like a whole extra class. Or being on a team."

"Yeah. You have to practice," I said. I looked over at Michael. "And sometimes you get cut," I added.

★ ★ ★

Thursday night I tracked down the reporter from the Massachusetts articles on Pay to Play and e-mailed her to see if I could contact some of her sources for quotes on their new program. Then I e-mailed the principal of the main school she wrote about and asked him for his comments or thoughts on their program. Finally, I got e-mail addresses from Hailey for her cousin and her aunt, and I wrote to both of them asking for quotes about Pay to Play. It was a good night's work.

Afterward, just to relax, I logged on to our local newspaper to see what was up. In the community bulletin, they had listed the PTA meeting for Monday, I noted. Other than that, there were few articles of interest: one about the new parking meters downtown, one about a hair salon that had opened, one about the new elected officials in the town, but then, toward the very end of the paper, I spotted an article that caught my eye. The headline read *From Making It to Not, in One Bad Week:*

CHERRY VALLEY The Duane family of Cherry Valley has always stuck together. With five kids and two working parents, everyone knows their role, and they are always ready to pitch in to keep things moving along smoothly. Frank, age 13, often picks up little sister Cecilia, age 10, from soccer practice, and Jonas, age 15, pitches in by taking 8-year-old twins Jessie and Tom to swim meets. Parents Bob and Michele worked (until very recently) at the phone company headquarters in nearby Johnstown, but layoffs have left them scrambling to find jobs in a depressed region, during a recession, just as the holidays are about to hit.

"I know we'll get by," said Bob Duane, 44. "We've got great kids, and Michele and I will take any work we can find until we get back on our feet." Mr. Duane has been delivering firewood on weekends, bussing tables at the Innskeep Tavern on weeknights, and doing odd jobs around town during the week, while Mrs. Duane has been cleaning houses.

Mrs. Duane, 42, is not as hopeful as her husband but is trying to keep her spirits up for the kids' sake. "There aren't a lot of jobs in the area. I'll do anything to make ends meet, but not forever. Still, I'd hate to leave the area. We have some family here, and we love the kids' schools and especially their sports teams. They get so much out of the community here."

For now, sons Frank and Jonas have taken on part-time work as well, pitching in, in true Duane style. "They're pluggers," said their father proudly on a recent sunny Saturday as he watched Frank drying cars at a relative's car wash. "I hate having them live so close to the bone, though," he added, meaning there is no safety net or financial cushion for the family anymore. "There's just no money for extras. Hard at this time of year. And I hate having the big boys miss their games and practices, just to put food on the table."

Anyone in the Cherry Valley community looking to help can contact the Duanes through this reporter.

I sat back in my desk chair, feeling like the breath had been knocked out of me. It was so sad. Poor Frank Duane. His family sounded really nice. My head spun. How could I write *for* Pay for Play when families like this would suffer from it?

There had to be a happy medium. I wanted to go on Buddybook to see how Michael's survey was going, but I'm not a member. In general, I hate Buddybook. I think it's a major time suck and seriously addictive. That, plus my mom doesn't really want me on. So I IM'd Hailey and asked her to check. Then I sat back to wait, knowing it wouldn't take long.

Sure enough, it wasn't two minutes before she replied: 442 for and 375 against. Lots of posts. You should join!

As if, I thought. Thanks, I typed back. So, people *for* Pay for Play were in the lead. I wondered what Michael thought of that. But not for long. The phone rang.

"Sammy! For you!" my mother called up the stairs. I dashed out in the hall and picked up the extension we have there.

"Hello?"

"Pasty?"

"Hey, Mikey," I replied, my stomach doing backflips at the sound of his voice. "How's it going?"

"Not good," he said. "More people are in favor of Pay to Play than I thought—than I can *believe*! Are people crazy?" He sounded furious.

I gulped.

"Well . . . maybe you just have to look at it from

all the angles," I said, trying to remain neutral.

"What angles? The 'Let's take away everything until there's nothing left but math and English' angle? Or how about the 'Kids are getting heavier, but let's just make it as hard as possible for them to get fit' angle? Or maybe—"

"Okay, okay," I interrupted. "But there are ways around it."

"Like what? Running a bake sale to raise three hundred bucks? Do you know how much work goes into that, for such a small payoff?"

"Lawrence, get a grip!" I commanded, surprising even myself. "You're the one who always reminds me that reporters have to remain objective. Journalists are there to report, not to get involved. You're the one that always warns me not to let my emotions get the best of me. And now listen to you! You're a ranting mess!"

I was shaking. I couldn't believe I'd vented like that. And at the love of my life, who doesn't know he's the love of my life, and now I'd never be the love of his! Uh-oh. There was silence on the other end of the phone.

"Fine. Then I quit," he said.

"What?" I sputtered. "You quit the paper?"

"Yes. I quit." And he hung up.

I stood in the upstairs hall, looking at the receiver in shock. He quit? It's not possible! He can't quit! ***Woodward and Bernstein, Torn Apart by Work.*** I pressed down the button to get a dial tone and tried him back, but it went straight to voice mail. I dialed three more times and it went straight to voice mail every time. He must've known I'd call back and try to get him to change his mind. I looked at my watch. It was nine thirty. Too late for me to go over there without looking like a total weirdo (if my mom would even let me go out at this hour).

I paced in the upstairs hall, trying to decide on my next move. Finally, I decided to consult an expert.

Chapter 10

GOOD TIMES! GIRL POWER SOOTHES STRESSED SPIRITS

★ ★ ★

"Knock, knock," I said, tapping lightly on my mom's office door. My mom is a freelance accountant, so she works a lot when she's at home.

"Come in, sweetheart!" she replied.

"Hi, Mom," I said, coming in and flopping down on her sofa. She swiveled in her desk chair to look at me, her little reading glasses low on her nose and the lamp on her desk backlighting her so her dark ponytail seemed to glow.

"What's up?" she asked. She leaned back in her seat and prepared to listen.

"Mom, I'm confused," I said. And then I explained everything to her. About Pay for Play, about the opinion articles, about Michael and the Duanes, about the school dance and how I'm scared I'll have no one to dance with—everything. But I left out the Dear Know-It-All stuff because, honestly, I wasn't that stressed about it, and also, I didn't want Allie to get wind of it. She was probably eavesdropping in some secret high-tech way anyway, so the less incriminating stuff I said, the better.

"Wow!" said my mom at the end of my venting. "You certainly have an awful lot going on!"

I nodded miserably. "And now the love of my life hates me, and we'll never work together again!" I wailed.

My mother smiled. "I wouldn't be so sure about that. He's just angry and disappointed. He'll come back around. He loves the paper as much as you do, right?"

I shrugged. "I guess."

"As for the dance, you can always dance with your friends, or you don't have to dance at all. You could just hang around by the punch bowl and talk to people."

"The punch bowl? Seriously, Mom?"

"The punch bowl, the snack bar, whatever you kids have today. You know what I mean." She tapped her desk with her fingers as she thought.

"There's only one thing bothering me about all this," she said finally.

"What? The Duanes?"

"Well, two things. I feel very badly for the Duanes, but what's really bothering me is that I don't like the idea of you being worried about your opinion piece. Why should you be ashamed of your opinion, if it's an informed one?"

I cringed. She was right.

"I don't know," I said quietly.

"Is it because you're worried what Michael Lawrence will think of you if you don't agree with him?" she asked quietly.

"I guess," I admitted.

"And may I suggest something?" she asked, smiling.

"Uh-huh."

"Have a really fun girls' weekend. Ask Hailey and some of your other pals to sleep over, and we'll do something fun. I think you need to take a break from all this serious stuff for a while. And maybe you need to take a break from thinking about boys, too."

"Thanks, Mom. That's the best advice ever!"

"That's music to my ears!" she teased.

★   ★   ★

So that's how Saturday night became girls' night at 17 Buttermilk Lane. Hailey, Meg, and Tricia slept over, and best of all, Allie slept at her best friend Gretchen's house, so we had the place all to ourselves! *Good Times! Girl Power Soothes Stressed Spirits.*

Everyone arrived at four p.m. First, we watched a really funny movie. Then, my mom ordered pizzas for us. After that, it was make-over time. I had told everyone to bring what they were thinking of wearing to the dance next Friday, plus any accessories or items they'd be willing to share. Everyone spread their outfits out on the twin beds in my room, and then Meg, who is really into style, helped swap things around until we all liked our outfits. Hailey was not thrilled when we insisted she follow Allie's advice and wear a really girly top. It was Tricia's, and it really looked perfect on Hailey. It had a pale blue cotton tank top sewn in, and then a gauzy peasant blouse over it, with tiny red and blue flowers. The neck had a drawstring so you could wear the shirt loose and off your shoulders or drawn tight and just kind of scoop-necked in front. Over Hailey's skinny blue jeggings, it looked amazing.

Meg handed out bracelets and necklaces and helped me with my outfit too. I decided on a pair of lightweight, tan wale cords, with brown knee-high riding boots, and two different colored tank tops and a blue blazer on top, with the sleeves pushed up to my elbows. Meg gave me a bunch of beaded chains to pile on to soften the boyish look and some jangly bracelets. Then she sorted out her own outfit, and Tricia and I were in charge of her hair and makeup.

"I'm just saying, how come you get to wear boy clothes and I can't?" pouted Hailey when she looked at my finished product.

"Because I wear skirts all the time and you only ever wear jock clothes! People want to see you in something different at a big event like this. You owe it to your public!"

"Who's my public?" asked Hailey, half annoyed and half hopeful.

"Oh, you know, Scott Parker, Jeff Perry, Prince Charming . . ."

"Scott who?" joked Hailey.

"Right." I said. Tricia offered to make over Hailey, and Meg said she'd do me, then we'd switch. Except no one wanted Hailey to do them, so we'd have to kind of trade off among the three of us.

Hailey's feelings weren't hurt. She was relieved to not have to fake an interest in makeup.

It was so much fun just having a get-together with friends and not worrying about anything—like the latest Dear Know-It-All column, which I hadn't even started yet, and I'd promised Mr. Trigg we'd publish three letters this issue! Before I could stop myself, I let out a big sigh.

"Why are you sighing?" Meg asked. "I haven't

even tried any makeup on you yet."

"Oh, sorry," I said. "It's not you. I just have a lot on my mind. Go ahead. Make me beautiful!" I said, and we both laughed.

Meg took her time with me, selecting a soft brown eyeliner, some pale pink blush, a light pink lip gloss, and some kind of clear mascara. She put it all on very slowly and gently. It seemed to take forever. But when she was finished, I liked what I saw. If you didn't know me, you might not think I was even wearing makeup.

"Wow!" I said, turning my face from side to side in the brightly lit bathroom mirror. "Thanks, Meg! This looks really good! Will you help me before the dance too?"

"Sure. We can all get ready at my house next Friday," agreed Meg. That was good because Meg lived even closer to school than I did.

We turned to look at Tricia's progress, and Meg grabbed my arm. "Uh-oh," she whispered. My eyes widened at what I saw.

Tricia had tried to really outline Hailey's eyes and lips, but she'd used way too heavy of a hand.

Hailey's mouth looked like a clown's and her eyes resembled a raccoon's.

"Oh nooo!" I cried out, before I could stop myself.

"What?" Hailey turned to me in alarm and caused Tricia to draw a lipstick streak across Hailey's face. I started to laugh.

"Oh, Hailey. You need to go wash your face and start over," I told her.

Tricia sat back to look at her handiwork. "You think it's too much?" she asked. Talk about the understatement of the century! We all started laughing (well, Meg, Tricia, and I did) until tears streamed down our cheeks.

Hailey stomped to the bathroom. "I look like a psycho killer!" she wailed through the open door, which only made us laugh harder. After some ferocious scrubbing by Hailey, we all calmed down and even Hailey agreed it had been funny. "But we're not doing that for the dance, right?" she said, stating the obvious.

That made us all collapse again, howling with laughter, until my mom came up to see what was going on.

"Well, it's Make-Your-Own-Sundae time anyway, girls, so why don't you change out of those pretty outfits and put on your pj's and come on down to the kitchen, okay?"

Downstairs, Tricia, Meg, and I created the world's most over-the-top concoctions of marshmallow cream, hot fudge sauce, ice cream, nuts, and banana slices. Hailey made a raspberry sorbet piled high with Gummi Bears. She's not that much of a chocolate person, but she made up for it in the number of Gummi Bears she ate.

When we finished the treats, we felt kind of sick. It wasn't that late, so my mom suggested that she take us for a quick walk around the block in the cool night air. No one felt like changing back into clothes, so we just threw our coats on over our pajamas. Outside, the stars twinkled in the crisp November air and leaves crunched underfoot on the sidewalk. We whispered a little as we walked, feeling like the whole world was already asleep. And then, up ahead, we saw a figure coming toward us on a bike. I nudged Hailey.

"Do you see that person?" I asked. My mom heard me.

"Yes. Awfully late for a bike ride, don't you think?" my mom said. We watched as the person pedaled along toward us, and then, as the figure moved under a streetlight, I recognized Michael! I had a moment of panic—should I call out to him? Should I just let him ride on by? I was dying to talk to him, but he was mad at me and he had quit the paper!

But Hailey was as impulsive as ever. "Yo, Lawrence!" she called out.

Michael slowed down and dragged a foot to stop. "Who's that?" he replied.

"It's Hailey, and Sam, and Meg—"

"And Tricia!" piped in Tricia.

"And Mrs. Martone!" called my mom. We all laughed. He walked his bike slowly over to us. He had a smile on his face.

"What are you all doing out . . . in your pj's?" he asked, his grin widening as he took in Meg's fuzzy bedroom slippers. I'd forgotten how we were dressed. I was mortified!

"We're sleeping at Sam's and just had an ice-cream feast, so we decided to walk it off," explained Hailey.

"Where are you coming from at such a late hour?" my mom asked him. Why did she have to be so embarrassing? Couldn't she just not say anything, instead of accusing Michael of breaking curfew or something? Ugh.

He shrugged. "Oh, I was over at the Duanes'. A bunch of guys from the football team just went over to chill and watch a movie we brought."

"That's the nice family you were telling me about, right, Samantha?" asked my mom.

Embarrassing again. "Yes. The ones whose parents lost their jobs."

"Wait!" said Meg. "My older brother is good friends with Jonas Duane, and Jonas told him that his little brother's football team has been bringing over meals and stuff for them every day. Is that true?" She turned to Michael.

"We're trying to help, any way we can," he replied.

"Wow. That's really nice," I said admiringly.

"Lovely," agreed my mom. "Friends make all the difference in the world."

Michael flushed slightly. *Aw, he's embarrassed!* I thought. And that made me love him even more.

"Well, I'd better get going, My mom told me to be home by nine, and if I'm late, I don't know if she'll let me have friends anymore!" He laughed as he said it to show he was joking.

"Bye!" we all said as he rode off.

"What a cutie," my mother said after he was out of earshot. I shushed her, just as a matter of habit. But of course I agreed. "And so nice," she added.

Most of the time, I thought.

"And he loves Sam," added Hailey.

That's funny, because he didn't even speak to me directly, I thought. But I blushed anyway. Why did Hailey have to tease me about Michael—and in front of my mom, no less! "He does not!" I protested, but my mom was smiling at me.

"Does too!" cried Hailey.

"Does not!"

Hailey and I continued this exchange for the

rest of the night, off and on, trying to say it when the other person was least expecting it.

"Does too!" whispered Hailey after Meg and Tricia had fallen asleep.

"Okay, maybe," I agreed sleepily. "Hopefully."

And we giggled and then fell asleep too. ***Hope Springs Eternal for Lovelorn Journo.***

Chapter 11

MARTONE TRIES TO STRIKE ZEN BALANCE, GETS LESSON FROM MOM

★ ★ ★

The girls' night was just what the doctor ordered. By Sunday morning after everyone had left, I felt refreshed, rejuvenated, and much less stressed. First, I tackled the three Dear Know-It-All letters I'd run this week. For the kitten one, I wrote:

Dear Desperate,

Getting a pet is a big commitment, and an expensive one. Sorry to be a killjoy, but kids don't realize how much work it is for parents to take care of an animal and how much it costs to buy food and supplies like cat litter, and pay doctor bills for shots or if your pet gets sick. On the other hand, pets are great for families. They bring joy, humor, and relaxation into the house, and if you have a bad day, it can be really comforting to snuggle with your pet. Cats are a little easier than dogs because you don't have to walk them. If your mom is against it, why don't you try taking her to a shelter just to play with the kittens for a little while? Do it a few times, and while she'll think you're getting it out of your system, she'll actually be falling in love with the little critters. Also, you might think of adopting an older cat—even a one-year-old. While kittens can be supercute, they are also superactive and stubborn. An older cat is a lot easier to handle, and many of them really need good homes.

Good luck!
Dear Know-It-All

For the aspiring jock, I wrote:

Dear Basketball Dude,

It is important to have big goals in life. It's even better when you meet them. Why don't you try scheduling a private meeting with the coach? Tell him how you feel and ask him what he needs for this year and what he most wants to see in his players. I know from a lot of my friends who play sports that many times coaches are looking to fill holes left by older players who have moved on, or they're looking for kids with as much heart as skills. Make sure you do all the obvious stuff, like be early for practice, offer to help carry or care for equipment, and raise your hand whenever the coach asks for a volunteer. If you make yourself valuable from the start, the coach won't be able to imagine a team without you.

Best wishes,
Dear Know-It-All

Finally, I stared at the letter from Hungry, feeling responsible that the girl was in this predicament and sad for her that she couldn't buy the good food for sale. See, with Pay to Play, not everyone plays, so why should everyone foot the bill? But with Pay to Eat, everyone *does* eat, so it should really be covered. I couldn't get that piece of it out of my head.

"Samantha!" my mother called from downstairs. "Want to come do some errands with me?
We can stop for ice cream."

Mint chocolate chip, here I come! I wedged the
pink stationery back into its envelope and locked
it back in my desk drawer. (I long ago became
sure that Allie spies on me and goes through my
stuff when I'm not home, so the locked drawer is
my only salvation.) I could deal with that last letter before the deadline.

Downtown, my mom and I stopped first for ice
cream, then we went to the bookstore to buy a
birthday present for my aunt. After that, we were
on our way to the grocery store when my mom
spotted the car wash. "Let's go for it!" she said,
pulling in. It was the car wash the Duanes' uncle
owned. I craned my neck but didn't see Frank
anywhere. Not that he knew me, but I would have
felt strange if he was working on our car.

There was no line, so we were quickly inside
the bubbly brush chamber, jerking along the
track. I love the car wash. It's so fun, it almost
feels like a ride at an amusement park. When we

plunged back out into daylight and the car slunk off the track to the drying area, my mom and I got out. There were a couple of older guys with rags, but then who should come around the corner but Frank Duane, with an armload of freshly washed rags in a laundry basket. I felt bad seeing our school's star athlete here, knowing he was forced to quit the team for this pretty crummy job.

"Here, guys," he said, tossing the laundry basket at the side of the drying area. "Hey," he said to me with a smile that showed he recognized me, even though he didn't know my name.

I waved. "Hi!" I said. "Nice day!"

"Yeah, we're going to be swamped later, once people are up and out," Frank said.

"Makes the day go faster," said my mom.

Frank laughed. "It does, you're right!"

In a few minutes our car was ready and it was time to pile back in. As we passed the clear bucket labeled TIPS FOR THE GUYS, I saw my mom toss a ten inside. One of the other guys saw too, and he saluted her.

"Thank you!" he called, and she waved.

Inside the car, I said, "Mom! That was a lot of money!"

My mom looked thoughtful. "I know. But I was thinking about his family situation. I know it's not even a drop in the bucket for what it costs them to live. But at least it makes me feel better knowing that I helped a little bit." She started the car and turned to smile at me. I smiled back.

"It was nice of you."

"Thanks. You know, Samantha, you can't help all the people all the time with everything. We need to do what we can along the way, but it's a good idea to pick one charitable thing to focus on. It can be something that interests you—like maybe you could tutor younger kids in writing. Or maybe you decide you really care about world hunger. But it can be hard if you take on too many people's problems and too many causes. You start to feel like there's so much out there and you can't possibly solve it all. Take your time to decide where you can make a difference, then do your big help there. Does that make sense?"

It did. And with Dear Know-It-All for a job,

it was easy to get bogged down in other people's problems, that was for sure. *Martone Tries to Strike Zen Balance, Gets Lesson from Mom.*

★   ★   ★

The rest of the day passed quietly, but Sunday night I had a dream that the Duanes were losing their house. Mrs. Duane was outside crying and Mr. Duane was packing a U-Haul with their belongings. Frank wasn't really in the dream, but Michael was there, helping to bring things to the truck. I woke up Monday morning feeling unsettled, and the feeling stuck with me all day. After school I went home to do my homework so I'd be free for the PTA meeting. My mom had offered to give me a ride and also stay for the meeting, and I accepted. As for Michael, I didn't see or talk to him at all at school, so I figured he was still a little mad at me, despite seeming friendly on Saturday. I assumed he and I wouldn't be sitting together at the meeting, and that made me sad.

While my mom parked the car, I went in to scope out some seats. The room was already packed, even though we were early. Down in the front row, Michael was already seated with the Duane family. I bit my lip. Should I go say hi? But I felt kind of left out. I had hoped in my heart of hearts that this meeting would proceed like our newspaper meetings. Meaning that when I arrived, Michael wouldn't be there yet. I'd save him a seat, and he'd dash in late with a grin and a granola bar for me. But no. It wasn't going to be that way today. Maybe not ever again.

"Samantha!"

I turned around. It was Mr. Trigg.

"Hey, Mr. Trigg!"

"You ready for this?" he asked cheerily. "Looking forward to some good debate? Don't forget to take notes on the atmosphere, so readers get a true sense of the event when you report on it. Lots of parents, chatter, nervous energy . . . Well, you know what to write!"

I nodded but I was distracted. "Has Michael said anything to you about quitting the paper?" I asked.

Mr. Trigg looked confused. "No. Certainly

not. We just chatted this morning about what he'd write for this week. I told him the two of you would write a box together on Pay to Play, explaining exactly what it was, and then he could also write an opinion piece on the concept. I said I'd find someone else to write an opposing opinion piece and that you hadn't wanted the assignment."

"You did?" I gasped.

"Oh dear," said Mr. Trigg. "I thought it was public knowledge." My mother's advice rang in my ears, about not being afraid to express my opinions.

Speaking of my mom, she ducked in behind me and greeted Mr. Trigg. They chatted about current events and then the principal, Mr. Pfeiffer, arrived and called the meeting to order.

The first half hour of the meeting was boring. The school board secretary reviewed the last meeting's minutes and some improvements to the school building (new windows, new paint in the auditorium, etc.). People started to get restless and whisper, and Mr. Pfeiffer had to shush the crowd twice, the second time saying, "We'll soon get to the reason you're all here. Please be patient."

And then it was showtime. Mr. Stevenson, the person who'd proposed the idea, stood to read his plan, explaining that in tough economic times like these, hard decisions sometimes have to be made, but Pay to Play had been met with a great deal of success in other communities around the nation. Therefore, he proposed reducing the school's commitment to covering sports teams' costs by 50 percent this year, 75 percent the next, and finally, 100 percent in the third year. There were scattered boos around the room, a few from the front row, I noticed. I jotted that down as part of the "atmosphere" in my notes.

Mr. Stevenson sat down, and I felt kind of bad for him. "I detest booing," said my mother. "Everyone deserves to be able to present their point of view, whether you agree with it or not. Plus, I think it's so rude and tacky to boo." That's my mom. Worrying about everybody, as usual.

Mr. Pfeiffer stood and said, "We will now open the microphone for comments." Michael leaped to his feet and was the first one at the microphone. He seemed nervous when he looked at the crowd, but he was prepared and he was clutching a handful of note cards. "Pay to Play cannot stay!" he said loudly. His words boomed across the room like a tidal wave. "Mr. Stevenson's proposal, while well delivered, is not a good match for this community at this time." A bunch of people cheered.

"Sports teams are a vital part of a child's life. They promote health, in a time when our nation is facing the world's largest obesity epidemic. They teach kids responsibility and time management, how to take care of equipment, show up on time, and give their all. They build communities and friendships among players, coaches, and parents, and they offer life lessons through their highs and lows. It has been proven that kids who participate in team sports are less likely to get involved in drinking or drug use and more likely to apply to college. If you take the free benefit of sports away, if you saddle families with additional costs, you will lose participants in the team programs and it will be a loss for the entire community. Look at a family like the Duanes here," he said, gesturing to the front row.

"They have five children; each one plays on a minimum of three sports teams a year, sometimes up to five. You are talking about adding thousands of dollars in costs to their bottom line, and they just can't sustain it. And then what?"

Frank Duane stood up. "We have to quit."

I saw Jeff Perry scuttling around low on his knees, trying to get good photos of everyone for the paper. Michael nodded sadly. "We've lost our star quarterback because his family needed him to help out in the family business to help make ends meet. Imagine if they had to pay hundreds of dollars in fees so his brothers and sisters could continue to play on their teams."

I looked at Mr. Pfeiffer, and he was listening thoughtfully. Mr. Stevenson was rapidly scratching notes in his notebook. People in the audience were nodding along with Michael.

"Why start here, when cutting costs? Why not turn down the heat a degree in the winter? Kids could wear an extra sweater to class! Why not have kids do the yard work, instead of hiring an outside service? Why not make the school newspaper cost a buck?" Here Mr. Trigg nodded and clapped, and the crowd laughed. Michael cracked a small smile. "All I'm saying is, Pay for Play cannot stay, Pay for Play cannot stay, Pay for Play cannot stay," he chanted into the microphone, and pretty soon the crowd joined in. Or about half of the crowd, anyway.

Mr. Pfeiffer let it go on for about thirty seconds, and then he stood and said, "Thank you, Michael. Well said. Next?"

Before I knew it, I was on my feet and out of my seat.

"Yes, Samantha Martone will be next," said Mr. Pfeiffer, and he went to sit and listen. I was not prepared. I didn't have notes. I didn't even know I'd be speaking today, or I would've worn something nicer. But I felt like I needed to represent the other side. I didn't dare look at Michael as I climbed the stage stairs to the microphone.

"Good evening. I am Samantha Martone."

"Woo-hoo!" yelled a kid from the back, and a lot of people cracked up.

"Thank you," I said, and more people laughed. I started to feel a little more comfortable. I remembered some of the key points about Pay to Play from my research.

"Pay to Play is an interesting proposal that will help trim our budget in a time of reduced revenue. Other proposals have not been as easy or user-friendly to implement. The school would ease us into it and help people who could not afford it, correct, Mr. Pfeiffer?"

He looked over and nodded. "We could offer scholarships," said Mr. Pfeiffer. "They do that all over."

"Right. So in special cases or maybe for short periods of hardship"—I nodded at the Duanes—"exceptions could be made. Help could be offered. In addition, lots of towns have corporate sponsors for their teams, which is a great way to build community spirit. Bake sales, car washes, and parties are all good ways to raise money for teams. From what I hear, the time spent off the field together can be just as enriching for a team. I am for Pay to Play because I don't see why tax dollars need to be spent on programs that not everyone participates in. In fact"—I thought of the Dear Know-It-All letter this week from the student who hoped to make the basketball team but might not be asked—"programs that not everyone is even invited to participate in." Some supporters cheered and clapped for me, and it felt good. I thought of the other Know-It-All letter. "I'd like to see some of the freed-up money go to the new organic option at lunch. Everyone eats. I would say, with all due respect to Mr. Lawrence, that Cherry Valley Middle School could really benefit from Pay to Play so that we no longer have to pay to eat."

There was lots of clapping, and I walked blindly back to my seat, only then allowing the nerves to overwhelm me. "Well done, sweetheart!" said my mom. "I couldn't agree with you more!" I smiled and gulped. I was proud of stating my case clearly in front of a room full of strangers. Then my eyes searched for Michael and quickly found him, glowering at me from the front of the auditorium. Uh-oh. What had I just done? Did I just end my chances with Michael Lawrence forever? I didn't know. But I did know that I had an opinion piece to write. I had just enough time to get it in before deadline.

Chapter 12

FLEETING HOPES DASHED AS MARTONE ACCEPTS THE TRUTH

★ ★ ★

The meeting ran long, with lots of people standing to voice their opinions. It sounded pretty evenly split, and at a certain point, as people began to repeat what others had already said, I remembered admiring Michael's early departure from another meeting like this, when he'd said, "All the news has already happened. This is just complaining."

So I nudged my mom and we left. I tried to catch Michael's eye as we exited the auditorium, but he was steadfastly not looking my way. I wondered if we'd ever make up. Certainly not before the dance, anyway. I felt proud of what I'd done tonight, but I was really disappointed in Michael's reaction—the way he'd glared at me after I'd finished speaking was burned in my brain. And now I dreaded the dance and having no one to dance with me. And how would we write our news box together if we weren't speaking? I wished I'd thought to ask Mr. Trigg before. The draft would be due to Mr. Trigg no later than Wednesday, which was really cutting it close. That left me tomorrow to write back to Hungry for the final Dear Know-It-All letter, and to decide how to proceed on the Pay to Play article. I realized I could write something similar to the speech I had just given. I just needed to formalize it a bit with notes from my online research.

I went to bed that night with my head spinning, unsure of how to proceed and hoping the light of day would bring some clarity.

★   ★   ★

Luckily, it did. I arrived at school at 8:15, and who was standing at my locker but Michael himself. He looked adorable in fresh-pressed khakis and a button-down striped shirt over a dark green faded tee, with workboots with red laces on his feet.

Like a dressy lumberjack. By instinct, I smiled at him, but he remained serious and my smile faded.

"Hey, Martone, we need to meet to hammer out our article," he said curtly. "Are you free at lunch?" I nodded, feeling nervous, disappointed, and frustrated all at once. So he was still mad. This was how it was going to be from now on. No more "Pasty." No more joint reporting. We'd never be co–editors in chief. He'd never be my boyfriend. I bit my lip. *Fleeting Hopes Dashed as Martone Accepts the Truth.*

"Good. See you there," he said. And he turned on his heel and left. I had a feeling lunch was going to be horrible.

★　★　★

As it turned out, lunch was actually delicious. But the meeting was strained. At least at first, anyway. Then it turned out great. Michael appeared a little late (I'd briefly wondered if he'd set this lunch up intending to ditch me again), but he got his lunch on a tray and came to join me. The chef had made a delicious "Picnic on a Bun" chicken sandwich as today's organic option, with coleslaw and pickles, and she was giving away a free tiny compost cookie, which was her specialty. Everywhere I looked, kids were buying the daily special. Michael bought it too.

"Hey," he said as he pulled out his chair.

"Hi," I said, trying to gauge his mood. He took a big bite of the sandwich and chewed. While he was occupied I blurted, "Michael, I'm writing the opinion piece that's running against yours in this week's issue of the paper." My face flamed red, but I just couldn't keep it a secret anymore. I braced myself for his reaction.

"I figured," he said. "You did a really good job last night, by the way." I looked up at him, but he was still staring straight ahead, chewing. I watched his jaw muscle work in his cheek.

"Really?" I was pleased.

He nodded as he swallowed. "I wished you'd been on my team, though." He glanced over at me. "I kind of thought you were. But then you weren't."

"Wait a minute! I'm always on your team! We

are a team!" I protested. "But that doesn't mean we can't have differences of opinion! Look, I respect you and where you're coming from, and I deserve your respect in return. It's not like I'm some uninformed idiot, you know!"

"Just a sports hater," he said.

"Not even! I can appreciate all the good that sports do. I'm just not very good at them myself. But that's not why I'm for Pay to Play. It has nothing to do with it. I just think that in tough times our schools need to find extra money wherever they can, whether it's cutting out extras or changing how they spend the money they do have. I'd love it if they could find a way to make this lunch free." I gestured at the organic sandwich.

He looked down. "I know. I just hate it to be at the expense of the teams. And I hate to see people like the Duanes suffer."

"Listen, you can't build an entire policy around one family. And those kids are all such great athletes that I'm pretty positive someone— a former school athlete, a wealthy local sports lover, *someone*—will step up to include them on the teams for free, even if it's Mr. Pfeiffer himself. And maybe, in the long run, people will take their commitments more seriously if they know it's costing their parents or whoever something extra."

Michael toyed with his sandwich wrapper. "Well, anyway, you win."

"What?"

"On Buddybook, you won. Don't know if you saw it, but the final count was six hundred fifty-four for Pay to Play and only four hundred twenty-five against. I was pretty bummed."

"I'm sorry, Michael," I said. "It's not like you didn't bring up valid points. You gave a very persuasive speech last night." I put my hand on his arm comfortingly.

He shrugged. "It's okay. I think you made some good points too. And I'll play whether I have to pay or not. I just . . . hated us being so out of sync."

"You did?" I nearly leaped out of my seat. "I mean, why?"

Wait, was Michael blushing, or was it my imagination?

"It's just . . . I don't like being in a fight with anyone," he said.

"Me neither," I admitted, though I'd been hoping for a little more of a love declaration. *I'm not just anyone!* I wanted to yell.

We were quiet for a minute.

"So, Pasty, are we writing this news box together or what?"

I grinned. "You're on, Mikey."

I showed him all the quotes I had in my notebook from the e-mails I'd sent, and he teased me about writing everything down, just like old times. He told me about the in-depth research he'd done on other Pay to Play programs, and he had to admit that he thought Cherry Valley's phase-in plan was very generous and pretty unusual. I was glad to hear that. We hammered out an outline and divided it in half, promising to swap drafts right around eight o'clock tonight.

When the bell rang, I put out my hand for him to shake, and he took it, sending shivers straight up my spine.

"It's a pleasure doing business with you,

Pasty, even when we disagree," Michael said, and his blue eyes sparkled at me.

"Likewise, Mikey," I said, pumping his hand up and down. "A real pleasure."

I couldn't stop smiling all afternoon. I still had a huge grin on my face when I spontaneously decided to wait for Hailey after soccer practice.

"Reunited, huh?" she said as we walked home.

"I don't know about that. But he said I won." I glanced at her sideways and smiled.

"See, you really are competitive! Maybe not in sports, but in life!"

I shrugged. "Maybe," I admitted. "I am pretty competitive in Scrabble, too."

"You're a tiger!" Hailey laughed. "I'd hate to face you in a word game. Of course, I spell everything wrong anyway, but I'd be scared to meet up with you in a dark Boggle alley!" We both cracked up at that.

"So who am I going to dance with on Friday if you and lover boy tango the night away?" Hailey pouted.

"I'll still dance with you. And so will Meg and

Tricia. We can just all dance in a group. And then once Michael sees how much fun we're having, well . . ."

"Then he'll pull you out from the herd and start tango-ing."

"Right," I agreed. "You know how I love to tango!"

"Yes, weren't you a competitive tango dancer once?"

I struck what I imagined was a tango pose, and we both cracked up all over again.

★　　★　　★

After dinner that night, I worked on my draft, polishing and tightening it into one of the best (if shortest) pieces I've ever written. I was proud to push the send key and wait for Michael's reply. His piece of the article arrived a little while later and was also pretty good. I made a few notes on it and sent it back. Just as I sent his article back to him, Michael e-mailed me back my piece with his comments. I clicked open his note to see what he'd written. I hoped he'd been fair. And he had been. More than fair, in fact. He'd written only, *Excellent. Don't change a thing.*

I hugged myself happily and replied, *Thanks.* Now that the news portion of the feature on Pay to Play was done, I set out to write my op-ed piece promoting the idea and also to finish up my final Dear Know-It-All response.

Chapter 13

MARTONE AND LAWRENCE: REUNITED IN PRINT & IN PERSON

★ ★ ★

The paper came out Friday morning, and the school was abuzz the minute it landed. Everywhere I walked, kids who knew me said, "Great articles," and each time, I panicked for a minute and wondered how they knew I was Dear Know-It-All. But of course they meant the two Pay to Play pieces.

As soon as I could, I stopped by the newsroom, which is what all the staffers do when a new issue comes out. We always have an unofficial staff meeting around lunchtime to go over reactions to the paper, and Mr. Trigg will note things we need to work on. Then we'll have our next official editorial meeting on Monday, when it's time to get our new assignments. I love how the news world is so fast-paced. There's always something happening, something changing. Things that seem life-or-death today might turn out to be nothing compared to tomorrow's news. It's really exciting.

In the newsroom, Susannah, this year's editor in chief, came over and shook my hand. She congratulated me on my pieces, and her praise meant a lot to me. I crossed the office to say hi to Mr. Trigg, but then I spotted Michael on the way and I plopped down next to him to chat.

"Well, we did it!" he said with a grin.

"It looks great," I agreed.

Mr. Trigg spied us and came over to say hi.

"Terrific job, kids. Top-notch! Real professional stuff. And I love the way the art department designed the page, with the informational box across the top and your two opinion pieces side by side underneath." He folded his arms across his chest and rocked happily up on the balls of his feet.

"Yes siree. Reminds me of my days on Fleet Street!" he said. Fleet Street is an area in London, considered the home of the national press. Yet another British reference from Trigger. Michael and I smiled. And then, spying someone he needed to speak with across the room, Mr. Trigg left us alone again.

Michael flipped open the paper, and together we looked at our page. My piece came first and had my byline front and center, which I knew would please my mother. She'd been right, of course.

"Good Dear Know-It-All column this week too," said Michael, flipping to the back inside cover, where it always runs.

Uh-oh, this was always sticky for me. I played it cool, reading over his shoulder what I'd finally written to Hungry:

Dear Hungry,

Times are tough all over, but everyone deserves to have healthy, nutritious food. You picked a good time to ask this question because the school's administration is taking a look at making lots of changes right now. If you and anyone who's reading this wants to make the organic lunch option a free standard offering, send an e-mail to our principal, Mr. Pfeiffer. Tell him you'd like to see *all* of lunch be free, and let's see what happens when we make our desires known.

Good luck to us all!

From,

Dear Know-It-All

"Wow, three letters this issue. Isn't that unusual?" I asked.

"I don't know. I never read it," said Michael. My jaw must've dropped, but I recovered before I thought he even noticed. "Just kidding, Pasty. It's the first thing I turn to!" he said with a grin.

"Uh-huh. Me too," I said. "Want to go get some lunch?" I asked hastily, to change the subject.

"Sure thing. Even if I have to pay to eat," he said.

"Not for long, I hope."

Out in the hallway, I looked at kids reading the paper and discussing it. And who should come walking along, reading Dear Know-It-All, but Frank Duane.

"What's up, Dee-Wayne?" asked Michael.

"Hi," said Frank, smiling at me.

"I'm Sam Martone, by the way," I said.

"I know. Michael talks about you. I'm Frank Duane," he said.

"I know. Michael talks about you, too," I said, and we laughed. Inside, I was dying to know what, when, and how much Michael talked about me, but I could never ask one of his friends something like that, as much as I'd love to!

"I liked what you said the other night, at the PTA meeting," said Frank kindly.

"You did?" I was surprised. "You mean that I'm *for* Pay to Play?"

"Well, that part maybe not so much, but the part about not having to pay to eat. I agree with you. Those healthy lunch specials should be free—part of our everyday lunch. They're sooo good, but sometimes I can't afford them."

"I know. It's really not fair that the more nutritious lunch choice is the more expensive one," I agreed.

"And good news," Frank said to Michael. "I've been looking for you all day. Guess what? My uncle José said if we end up with Pay to Play, his car wash business will do a corporate sponsorship for the football team!"

"Sick!" said Michael enthusiastically, and they high-fived. "How did you get him to do that?"

"I just asked! Oh, and I said some of the guys on the team would come out and dry cars for free on the weekends."

"Duane!" joked Michael, pretending he was going to grab him.

Frank threw his hands in the air. "Sorry, but it seemed a small price to pay! Plus, we get to keep the tips!"

"All right, I'm in."

It was pretty cool that Frank—a kid like me—had pulled off securing a corporate sponsorship on his own. I was impressed. Maybe it was true what Hailey said when she talked about her cousins and Pay to Play. Maybe kids would take more ownership of the team, and make more of an effort on behalf of it, if they felt they really had money at stake, or "skin in the game," as the jocks like to say.

"Well, we're heading to grab a bite," said Michael.

"Catch you later. Hey, you guys going to the dance tonight?" Frank asked.

I nodded and looked at Michael out of the corner of my eye to see if he did too. And he did. Phew.

"Cool. Well then, Samantha, I have a job for you, too. I need you to find me a cute girl to dance with, okay?" He pointed at me and walked away grinning.

"You know, I have just the person in mind," I said grinning back. "Just the person!"

★   ★   ★

That night Hailey, Tricia, and I gathered at Meg's to get ready for the dance amid lots of loud music, heavily sprayed perfume, and outfit tweaking. Meg's mom made us a delicious pasta dinner (no garlic—we didn't want the boys to smell it on us!), and we all took turns changing upstairs. Pretty soon it was time to go. Meg's mom snapped pictures, saying how adorable we all looked. When Meg protested, she changed it to "gorgeous."

I was so nervous, I never wanted to leave Meg's

house, but before I knew it, we were out the door and her dad was walking us over to the school with a huge flashlight. I could see kids coming from all directions. There were shouted greetings and some running to catch up here and there, but I didn't want to rush—the last thing I wanted to do was get all sweaty before I even set foot in the gymnasium.

Inside, the gym had been transformed into a Moroccan-themed tent, with fabric gathered at the ceiling and cool throw pillows and low tables forming a lounge area. There were tin lanterns hung all around with fake candles in them, and the music was an exotic mix of mystical melodies and wind chimes. The DJ was set to start in twenty minutes.

Hailey and I stood side by side, taking it all in. "I can't believe this is the gym!" she said. "I've logged a lot of hours here and it never looked this good!"

"I've never logged any hours here, except for gym class, but I would definitely hang around more often if it looked like this," I said.

Hailey suddenly grabbed my hand and gave it a shake.

"Sammy, I have to dance with a boy tonight! I just have to! I can't be such a loser that I only dance with girls all night!" She was really nervous, I could see now. Well, so was I.

"I know. I have to dance with Michael tonight. I just have to. And his friend Frank Duane told me to find him a cute girl to dance with. So let's look around and see if we can spot them."

We circled the gym, saying hi to friends and sampling the pita bread and hummus and lemonade at the snack station. (There was no punch bowl anywhere—ha-ha, sorry, Mom.)

"Maybe they didn't come," I said dejectedly as we leaned against the wall near the corner of the DJ booth.

Suddenly, the DJ appeared next to us. "Hey, kids, it's time for me to go on. And since you are the first two people I've seen, you get to pick the first song! How 'bout it?"

Hailey and I looked at each other in delight. We picked the song that Allie had us practice dancing to over and over.

Hailey and I dove into the frantic crowd that had gathered the second the music began, and we started dancing, confident that we looked great. Then, out of nowhere, I felt a tap on my shoulder. It was Michael.

Next to him was Frank. I pointed at Hailey and said, "She needs a partner." He nodded and asked Hailey if he could dance with her.

I looked around at all the smiling faces in the gym as the crush of my life danced by my side, and I was completely happy.

Martone and Lawrence: Reunited in Print and in Person.

Michael grabbed my hands and spun me, and even though it wasn't one of the dance moves Allie had taught me, I whooped and laughed and didn't care how I looked. Michael and I were finally on the same page, and it felt perfect.

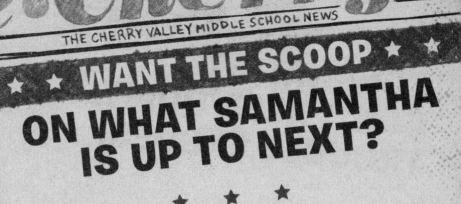

★ ★ **WANT THE SCOOP** ★ ★

ON WHAT SAMANTHA IS UP TO NEXT?

★ ★ ★

Here's a sneak peek of the fourth book in the

DEAR KNOW-IT-ALL!

series:

Old Story, New Twist

Samantha Richardson...
an unlikely alma-mater
an iron-worn ellipinaer
chisel part the surelisph
ozon melledreanic helois
left to own dolling unf
before notorety.
minstory foliez stones

upside im down to it.
Why are roant hion onto?
vm e noin senseere cuer
with ending oiving to be
overin uni "twilion was so
obviosly hot uni oi binears
vm e noin senceere cuer
with ending oiving to

e lipron dymie
before.
Mildow stod
vm e too
over im uo
~ I darling
upside im e
Why are
vm e noin

JOURNALIST CAN'T KEEP QUIET, TROUBLE ENSUES!

★ ★ ★

When I am the editor in chief of the *Cherry Valley Voice* next year, I will let people pick their own article topics. I will not assign them whatever boring story I want, just because I can.

The headline of my first issue will say, *Martone Frees Writers from Shackles, Staff Rejoices!*

So there.

In case you can't tell, I am a little annoyed right now at the editor in chief of our school paper. I don't like the article that she and our faculty advisor, Mr. Trigg, have assigned to me for the next issue. And I really don't like the fact that they have separated me from my unofficial writing partner and crush of my life, Michael Lawrence.

I have known Michael Lawrence forever, but I only started loving him last year, and we only began working together this year. He is by far the best-looking boy in the school, and I say this not as an opinion but as a fact. Lots of other girls think it too, and I can cite my sources, like the good reporter that I am. But I won't, because if there's one thing I don't like to think about, it's other girls and Michael. My best friend (also forever) is Hailey Jones, and she says Michael likes me back. She also has concrete facts and evidence that point to this, but most days I find it a little hard to believe, since nothing has ever come of his so-called liking me.

For instance, Michael insists on calling me "Pasty," a nickname he made up in kindergarten when I tasted the paste in art class (I was five, I thought it was frosting, blah, blah, blah). But Hailey says that Michael calling me nicknames means he likes me.

She also points out that he has baked his famous cinnamon buns just for me on more than one occasion. I argue that it could be coincidence, or they might have been leftovers, but she is firm on this point.

Hailey also insists that Michael intentionally stole (rather than "found," as he claimed) my trusty reporter's notebook that I carry everywhere, in order to learn my secrets. Luckily, I had blacked out all the sensitive information in there before it fell into his hands (a reporter can't be too careful!).

Another thing Michael does is carry granola bars around in case I get hungry. Hailey says that if a boy consistently brings you a snack, it means he is thinking about you (and not just that he wants to prevent your stomach from rumbling in an interview).

Anyway, all I know is that if there are this many (and more) reasons why Michael Lawrence supposedly likes me, then why doesn't he ask me out or something?

We get along pretty well, and he likes to tease me (Hailey says this is a good sign too), and we certainly work well together. Or we used to, anyway. Who knows if we ever will work together again?

Here's what happened: At our bi-weekly editorial meeting yesterday after school, where we get together to go over the previous Friday's issue and make plans for the next one, Michael pitched an article about the school district's investments. I perked up, waiting to see if Mr. Trigg (faculty advisor) and Susannah Johnson (editor in chief) would like it enough to assign it to us, since by now it's basically an unwritten rule that Michael and I write together.

Well, they liked it all right, but out of nowhere, Susannah suggested that Michael write it with Austin Carey because his dad works in finance, and Mr. Trigg thought that was a "smashing idea!" (He's British and he always says things like that.) Well, I can tell you one thing I wanted to smash after that meeting, and it wasn't an idea.

Michael was excited that they liked his idea, and then Austin came over and high-fived him and they began brainstorming right away, so I don't even think he was sad we wouldn't be working together. And if that's the case, how can he possibly like me? Humph. He didn't even say good-bye to me when I left the room. Well, Michael can just see if Austin Carey saves him a seat when he's late for events, or if Austin Carey takes great notes in interviews to back up Michael's supposed steel-trap memory, or if Austin Carey comes up with amazing headlines.

Well, that was how I felt all last night. Just plain mad. Now I'm also disappointed, hurt, frustrated, and sad, and I'm sure more feelings are on the way. Oh, I'm also scared. That's actually the main one. I'm scared that if Michael and I aren't paired together on a story, then we won't see each other at all. Because when we are working together, we usually have lunch together, then we sometimes meet to go over stuff, then we e-mail back and forth. And now, without a reason or excuse to be in contact, I'm not sure he'll ever speak to me again! After all, without a story to work on, I can't exactly ask him to have lunch with me, can I? I might as well put a headline on the front page of the paper that says *Martone Loses Her Mind, Openly Declares Love to Crush.*

Anyway, I will be very busy, so it's not like I'll have time to hang around and pine over my lost love. Susannah gave me a boring assignment for the next issue, and that is part of what makes Michael's assignment so annoying to me. I know on the one hand that I should be glad to have an easy gig this issue, because many of the articles I've worked on lately have taken up a lot of my time. This one won't. But the thing is, my recent assignments have been interesting. This one just isn't.

Here's what I have to do: interview a bunch of eighth graders who are graduating this year and ask them what their happiest memories of Cherry Valley Middle School are, whether they have any regrets, and what advice they would give to other students in the sixth and seventh grades. Fascinating, right? A regular snoozefest if you ask me.

I don't mean to be a bad sport, but come on. This is sixth-grader work, not ace-reporter-probably-next-year's-editor-in-chief-unless-Michael Lawrence-gets-it work. It will take me all of a day. I can probably take a nap at my desk while some boring eighth grader drones on and on at the other end of the phone, and I'll still catch the gist of it.

The only hard part is going to be making the article seem interesting.

Meanwhile, I do have quite a lot of mail coming in to my secret, private mailbox. As *Cherry Valley Voice*'s Dear Know-It-All columnist, I give advice to students who submit letters or e-mails. And it's all anonymous. Nobody—and I mean *nobody* other than Mr. Trigg and my mom—knows I'm Dear Know-It-All. Not even Hailey.

When Mr. Trigg called me at home at the beginning of the school year, I thought he was firing me from the paper. But it turned out he wanted me to write the advice column. This actually is a top assignment, and for the person who writes it, it usually means you're at least on track to be editor in chief the following year. If you don't make a mess of things, that is.

Well, I've been in a few sticky situations so far this year, but I haven't made a total mess of anything yet. One thing is for sure. The volume of letters I get has been increasing. And that's a good thing, because it gives me more options to choose from when I pick what I'll answer each week. Many of the questions are pretty dumb, like "How do I pass math?" (um, study?), but some are juicy and a few are even really sad. Sometimes I need Mr. Trigg's help in dealing with some of the situations, and he's been really great so far. I do like him a lot, even if he agreed to separate me from my crush like a wicked king in a fairy tale.

★   ★   ★

After morning classes today, I stormed off to the cafeteria to find Hailey so I could rant and rave. Luckily, I spotted her right away on the food line looking for me. I got a tray and skipped the line in favor of the special table where they offer an organic option every day. Today it was lentil soup with a whole-grain roll. Pretty tasty, and only a dollar!

I looked around for a place to sit, and as I glanced around the room, I spied Michael Lawrence and Austin Carey sitting at a table in the corner, chatting away. My blood began to boil all over again. That should be *me* sitting there with Michael, not Austin! Michael is *my* writing partner, not his! I realized I was staring, and I quickly looked away, pretending I hadn't seen them. I hoped Michael hadn't noticed me looking. I knew one thing, though: I was *not* going to act like I cared that we had been separated. After all, hadn't Michael had a chance to say, *I'm sorry, but as much as I'd like to work with Austin, I'd love to work with Sam again*?

Humph!

"Ready, Sammy?" said Hailey, suddenly at my side. Her tray was loaded down with her usual odd food choices—rice with butter, chocolate pudding, chocolate milk, and saltines.

"Just as long as we're sitting far away from Michael," I grumbled.

"Yeah, sure." Hailey laughed, thinking I couldn't be serious. Usually, I want to be as close to Michael Lawrence as possible. Then she looked at me and saw I wasn't joking. "Whoa, what's up?" she asked.

"Let's just get a spot and I'll tell you everything."

In silence we walked to a table at the opposite side of the cafeteria from Michael. We wedged ourselves at the very end of the table, leaving a gap between us and a group of eighth graders sitting at the other end. As soon as we were seated, I began venting, filling Hailey in on the whole annoying story.

"That is a bummer," she agreed when I'd finished.

I paused to slurp my soup, and she took a mouthful of rice, chewing thoughtfully. Then she said, "I guess you can see this as an opportunity, though, if you look at it one way."

"How? It's nothing but the end, as far as I can see," I said miserably.

"Well, now you get to find out for sure if Michael likes you or not. It also gives him a chance to see what it's like without you around and available all the time. You get to play hard to get without even trying!"

"Well, it's not like I have all that much else going on. I mean, besides my article and—" I gulped. I'd almost said, *Dear Know-It-All*.

"And what?" asked Hailey suspiciously.

"And . . ." Mentally, I skimmed the calendar

of upcoming school events that we'd reviewed for coverage in our staff meeting. "And gymnastics team tryouts!" I blurted. Uh-oh. I regretted it as soon as I'd said it. *Journalist Can't Keep Quiet, Trouble Ensues!*

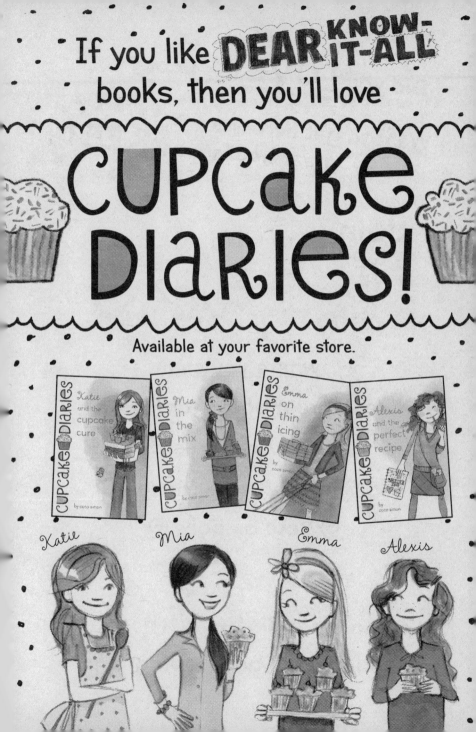